Puppy Pride

PRIDE CAMP 2025

GABBI GREY

J ai

Six years ago, the guy I thought I loved told all my friends that I liked to wear paws and a tail and crawl on the floor being a puppy. He turned my private play into a cruel joke, and I ran. Left my friends, my family, home, job, as well as my puppy-play group, and tried to let distance and time heal those wounds. Now, I've been given the chance to serve as the director of the new Mission City Pride Camp for teens. But my fresh start turns sour when someone starts leaving dog treats on my desk. Can I stand up to bullying this time and show these kids they have a right to be themselves? Or am I going to run again?

Demetrius

When my best friend got cancer, marrying her was the only real help I could give. Then she died, and I was left trying to single-parent my hurting stepson and stepdaughter without her. When Keegan tells me he's being bullied for being gay, I desperately want to help him gain resources to survive and thrive. Enrolling him at Pride Camp is step one, and I'm delighted to find the director is a pup I loved playing with back at Whatsup Pup Club. If anyone knows about being bullied and inner strength, it's Jai. I'd love to reconnect with him on a personal level, too, but he keeps pretending he doesn't recognize me. I figure leaving him reminder gifts is a good place to start, to show him I'm interested in man *and* pup. But he seems more and more stressed, and I wonder if I have it wrong. Is there any chance he'll let me be the Daddy I was for those short, sweet moments six years ago? Can I take a load off his shoulders, or will he shut me out forever?

Puppy Pride is an interracial, age-gap, hurt/comfort, second chance gay romance novel with a generous Daddy, a skittish pup, and the magic when they find each other again.

Welcome to Pride Camp, where diversity and inclusion is our motto. We've got daddies, mommies, littles, pets and families of all kinds. So, unroll your sleeping bag, make a couple s'mores, and enjoy the show!

Edits by ELF

Cover by Jo Clement

Dedication

Renae

Reshma

Wendy

TL

Jo

Kaje

ELF

Contents

1.	Chapter One	1
2.	Chapter Two	10
3.	Chapter Three	19
4.	Chapter Four	26
5.	Chapter Five	35
6.	Chapter Six	44
7.	Chapter Seven	53
8.	Chapter Eight	61
9.	Chapter Nine	68
10.	Chapter Ten	76
11.	Chapter Eleven	85
12.	Chapter Twelve	94
13.	Chapter Thirteen	103
14.	Chapter Fourteen	112

15. Chapter Fifteen   122

16. Chapter Sixteen   128

17. Chapter Seventeen   134

18. Chapter Eighteen   142

19. Chapter Nineteen   152

20. Chapter Twenty   164

21. Chapter Twenty-One   173

22. Chapter Twenty-Two   180

23. Chapter Twenty-Three   188

24. Chapter Twenty-Four   205

25. Epilogue   212

26. Interested in knowing more about Gabbi?   219

Chapter One

Jai

"We're going to have a great season." Cody gave me a reassuring smile. The warmth was echoed in his stunning blue eyes, under a mop of perfectly tousled curly, light-brown hair. Add a gorgeous six-foot-plus body and perfect teeth, and Cody could've been a high-fashion model instead of the psychologist at a summer camp for LGBTQ teens.

When I interviewed him, I'd worried about the kids crushing on him, or feeling like they couldn't measure up to his perfection. The camp therapist needed to be someone they could confide in, not someone they'd be desperate to impress.

Dr. Kennedy Dixon's recommendation overrode any concerns I might have. As one of Mission City's top psychologists, her word carried a lot of weight. She said Cody was perfect for the job, despite his young age. Or perhaps because of it.

"I wish I had your confidence," I told him. Still, I gave him the bravest smile I could. Mission City Pride Camp had been two years in the making and, for this inaugural season, everyone had high hopes.

No pressure.

"Everything will be fine." Cody was twenty-six, with his newly minted doctorate in clinical psychology earned at an almost unfathomably fast pace—much as Kennedy's had been more than ten years ago. Also, as he had pointed out in his interview, he had once been her patient. He had no qualms talking about his *rough period* where he'd been struggling with both coming out as gay and severe parental disapproval.

Kennedy saw him through that.

In turn, he dedicated his life to helping other teens. Hence cramming undergrad, a Master's degree, and his PhD into nine years of intense study.

He'd graduated three weeks ago.

I fretted. But then, as camp director, the man the founders hired to make their vision come true, I would always fret. "They'll start arriving in about twenty minutes."

"I'll make sure Makenna and Grey have everything they need. No worries, Jai. Everything will be fine." With a wave, he sauntered out of my office.

When Cody and I had met with Makenna and Grey—the two counselors—we'd had a discussion about titles.

Cody argued I should use my full name and expect to be Mr. Prasad.

Mr. Prasad was my father, and I hated to be reminded of him. *Should've changed your last name years ago.* Also, I was a mere three years older than Cody. Hard to believe since I felt a million years older.

Meanwhile, I'd mused whether Cody should use his PhD status since he'd graduated three weeks ago.

All three of the younger folks agreed that would put a barrier between Cody and the kids. Makenna and Grey, despite only being twenty-one, showed tremendous maturity.

Hence me hiring them.

I glanced out the window of my office in the administration cabin.

Pride Camp was made up of eight buildings—admin, cafeteria and main activities, female private cabin, male private cabin, nonbinary private cabin, two counselor cabins, psychologist cabin, and the camp director's private cabin. The founders of the camp spent a lot of time debating sleeping arrangements. The sleeping *cabins* were more like small dormitories—each camper got their own private bedroom and they shared the bathrooms.

The sound of a vehicle pulling up caught my attention.

I glanced at my watch.

Thirteen minutes early.

Sort of like something I would do. My first day, I'd been almost an hour early.

This camp was the brainchild of Smith and Alessandra MacLean. Alessandra had once been a social worker with community services and had witnessed firsthand elevated homelessness amongst the LGBTQ youth population.

She hadn't married Smith for his vast wealth—a fact she'd told me with a huge grin on her face—but she was happy to put his money to good use.

And he was delighted to encourage her.

They made their home in Mission City, and when this parcel of land on Stave Lake had gone on the market, they'd known what they wanted to do.

Two years later, here we were.

I stepped onto the porch and gazed over the parking lot.

A young man was getting out of an older-model minivan.

Keegan Mulroney. Probably the most tragic backstory of all our kids—and that was saying something. His father died in an industrial accident when he was still a toddler and his sister had been a newborn. Then, a few years ago, their mother died of cancer. Fortunately, Keegan's stepfather was, by all accounts, a great guy.

Since I was working on the assumption the man getting out of the driver's side was the stepfather, I was a little surprised.

Families come in all shapes and sizes.

Perhaps. But seeing a huge Black man placing a clearly comforting hand on Keegan's shoulder was unexpected. The thirteen-year-old was blond with crystal-blue eyes. Also, short and slender. At least a foot shorter than his stepfather.

If this is his stepfather.

I strode over to the two, arriving just as Cody did.

"Keegan? I'm so glad you're here." Our psychologist grinned.

"Yeah." The young man tried to hide behind his stepfather.

My heart sank.

"I'm Cody and I can help you get settled. Your counselor is Grey, who will be along in a moment."

"Counselor?" Keegan appeared to shrink in upon himself even further.

The large man beside him bent and met Keegan's gaze. "You remember the photos we looked at? Cody is the psychologist, and you talk to him about how you're feeling. He's your safe space."

"I don't know." Keegan broke eye contact and kicked at a pebble on the gravel driveway.

Cody held my gaze for a moment.

Before I could speak up, though, Keegan's stepfather continued. "And Grey is like a camp counselor. He's here to lead you through all the fun stuff you're going to do."

Keegan glanced up. "This is lame." His voice didn't hold defiance, though. More like painful resignation.

"I know you think that. But I *know* this is going to be good for you." The man smiled. "And they'll have your phone. If you need to talk to me, you ask nicely and they'll let you call me, any time. I'm staying in Mission City for the two weeks, okay? You need me, and I can be here in fifteen minutes."

"Why aren't you staying near Alaina?"

Alaina? Oh, the younger sister.

"Because she's on a trekking adventure through the forests on Vancouver Island. She's got, like, five adults with her."

"You mean she doesn't need you and I do."

Grey approached, but slowed when he caught my gaze.

I held up a hand to have him stay back for a bit. Keegan and his stepfather needed a bit of privacy—even though Cody and I were within hearing distance. This parting was tearing me up. And he wasn't my kid.

But I knew that kind of pain. From all indications, the stepfather was encouraging. *Should've double-checked the parents' names before coming out here.*

The kids I knew well, at least on paper. The parents? Not so much.

"There's nothing wrong with you needing me. And I can get to Alaina in a couple of hours, Keegan. You two are the most important people in my life. Don't ever—and I mean ever—doubt that."

Keegan met his stepfather's gaze. "Okay."

His stepfather glanced over at Cody and held out his hand. "Demetrius. This wonderful kid is my son." He beamed with pride.

"We'll take very good care of him, I promise." Cody beckoned Grey over. "This is Grey, and he'll be your counselor. He's around to make sure you have everything you need."

Grey stuck out his hand. "I was a camper a few years ago, so I know what it's like. Only I had to go to Ontario to find a camp for kids like myself. It's great we now have one so close to home. Where is your home? Do you want to follow me?"

"Vancouver." Keegan hesitated. "Uh, can I say goodbye to my dad?"

"Of course. We'll be over here. Oh, someone else is arriving." Grey waved to the incoming Mazda in need of a new muffler.

So I didn't hear whatever Keegan's stepfather said to him, but I did witness a hug so fierce that I had to blink back tears. Pride Camp was meant to be a place of acceptance and, hopefully, healing. Keegan was clearly in need of both. His dad had signed him up, alluding to ongoing bullying and *other issues* at school.

I'd sought elaboration from the school, but had hit a brick wall. Even with the stepfather's permission, the school stuck to the privacy policy. Deep in my gut, I believed they were protecting the privacy of the bullies. Quite often, that happened. Certainly more often than I'd like. More than was safe for the LGBTQ kids.

Keegan finally let go, grabbed his knapsack and suitcase, and followed Grey toward the boys' cabin.

Makenna was there to greet Luli, a petite Asian girl who was struggling as well. She also came from Vancouver. That said, we had several kids local to Mission City and Abbotsford who were slated to attend.

Cody hung back, clearly waiting for Makenna to make the introductions.

I'd planned to get into the mix, but I didn't want to overwhelm the kids. Better that I be off to the side, but available if needed.

Keegan's stepfather finally pulled his gaze from his retreating son's figure and pivoted his attention to me.

He blinked.

So did I. I'd glimpsed him upon their arrival, but had been more focused on Keegan. Now, though? I took a moment to catalogue the man. Tall. Well over my own five-eight. Broad. Barrel chested. Defined biceps under his T-shirt. Lean waist and thick thighs in straining khaki. His black hair curled, although it wasn't as long as my own. His dark skin glinted in the bright sunshine, and his dark-brown eyes mesmerized me. He was...stunning.

He cocked his head.

I stepped forward, extending my hand. "Jai Prasad. I'm the camp director."

"Demetrius Fulton." He grinned. "Your picture wasn't on the website."

"Oh." Of course, Alessandra's and Smith's photos weren't on the site either, and they were far more important. As I thought about it, though, mine probably should've been. We had a chef and an assistant in the kitchen. We also had a jack-of-all-trades guy who did the maintenance, as well as any cleaning that might be necessary. Everyone here had passed background checks. I'd hired each person myself, making sure we were all on the same page—which I believed we were. Their photos were all up.

"Uh, no picture. I'm not important around here. I'm very much in the background." *And I don't want it easy for my family to know I'm here.*

He frowned, even as he shook my hand. "That's absolutely not true. Alessandra sang your praises."

I cocked my head, weirdly disconcerted by how his grip was firm, but didn't overwhelm.

Finally, he released my hand. Then he smiled a little ruefully. "It's a very long story, but Alessandra runs an employee-assistance company. I called looking for counseling for both Keegan and myself after..." His voice trailed off. "I spoke to Hamish, a psychologist at the company. He mentioned this place was opening up and had Alessandra call me to see if Keegan might be a good fit."

Don't feel left out. You don't need to be consulted on everything. Or so I told myself. I thought I'd been brought up to speed on everything that had happened before I arrived, but clearly I'd missed something. Might not be important, but I filed it away as something to remember should the topic come up again. "Alessandra is amazing. She hired me."

"She said, when I spoke to her, that she had found just the right person. I'd say she found that person with you."

You don't even know me... "Thank you. I hope so. I do much of the administrative work, but I'm obviously here for the kids, should they need something. I'm also responsible for conveying any progress reports. Given the camp is only two weeks, I don't foresee there being many."

"Ah, sure." Demetrius glanced over his shoulder. "My kid's got...issues. I'm hoping Grey and Cody can cope—but I'm relieved to know you'll be here as well." He held my gaze.

"We're here to help kids with issues. Or without. I can't give private information, but I can say we have a wide and diverse group of campers. We're keeping it small this year as we find our footing, and we wanted a low camper-to-counselor ratio." *Which is way more than he needs to know and is all on the website. The website he clearly read.* "Well, you have my number. If you want to check in, don't hesitate to use it."

He grinned. "I won't. I look forward to seeing you again, Jai."

"That's great." Something about his smile sank deep inside me. I felt warm and fuzzy—and that never happened. I'd done romance once. Just once. Complete disaster. Never going there again.

And certainly not with the father of a camper.

What the hell are you thinking? Just because you find him attractive and he clearly loves his son... So much more than I *ever* got from my parents.

"Thank you." He offered possibly the widest smile I'd ever seen. Then he sauntered away.

As he drove away, two more cars pulled up.

Showtime.

Chapter Two

Demetrius

*B*uttercup.

My mind whirled a hundred miles an hour as I drove away from Pride Camp.

I'd found Buttercup. For six years, I'd thought about him and wondered how he was doing, and now…here he was. In Mission City. At the summer camp where I'd just dropped Keegan off.

Leaving my son was probably one of the toughest things I'd ever done. Well, my stepson. I didn't differentiate. My two adopted children might not have my blood, but they were mine in every single possible way that mattered.

I'm trying, Erlene. To give them the life you would've wanted for them. See? I even found someone to watch over your baby when I'm not there.

Well, like four someones. Makenna, Grey, Cody, and Jai. With Alessandra and Smith close by as well. I was sure they'd be intensely focused on making this inaugural camp successful.

I hummed as I drove the back roads from the northern rural outskirts down to Mission City proper. The town held fewer than forty thousand people. A blip compared to massive Vancouver where we lived. Where I'd lived for my entire life.

Slowly the trees began to thin, and I could see houses from the road. I turned onto Cedar Street, and soon I was passing townhouse complexes that appeared newer. Then I drove down the big hill that would take me to my hotel. I'd register, settle my stuff, and then head out to explore.

My friend Priscilla, upon learning I was heading to Mission City, insisted that I visit Fifties diner. Then she added Stavros's and a couple of other places to the list.

I'd kind of tilted my head, so she'd typed out a text with everything I needed to know. I was lucky to have good friends, but I wasn't here to be a tourist.

After turning left onto the main drag, I made my way to the Grand Hotel. The thing wasn't all that grand, but it had recently been renovated, and the pictures on the pretty website made it look warm and inviting. Since I was setting up for two weeks, the sight of ergonomic chairs in their executive suites appealed. That, and a large desk. Since I had two laptops running at all times, the extra space wasn't just a luxury—it was a necessity.

I parked, grabbed my suitcase, hefted my briefcase over my shoulder, armed the alarm on my car, and headed for the front door. Soon enough, I was inside.

"Welcome to the Grand Hotel." A pleasant female voice greeted me.

I yanked off my sunglasses and blinked several times. "Yeah, okay." I moved to the counter. "Fulton."

"Of course." The receptionist's megawatt smile didn't slip. "Fourteen nights, correct?"

"Yes."

"We have a special rate for guests who stay more than a week."

"Oh?" *I don't remember reading that. Oh well, score!*

"We don't always advertise the fact." A smooth, deep voice came from behind me.

I turned to find a handsome Black man headed my way.

He grinned. "I'm Aaron. I'm the manager."

"Demetrius." I extended my hand.

The man gave me a firm shake. "I have some level of discretion, and when I saw your reservation, I was happy to apply the discount."

"And I still get an executive suite?" I rolled my shoulder to gesture to my briefcase.

"Absolutely. Best internet connection we can provide. And we can plan housekeeping around your work schedule, so we're not disturbing you."

"Oh." Something I hadn't even considered—but super appreciated. "My hours are flexible. More like I've got a list of stuff I have to do in the next two weeks, and the sooner I finish, the more time I have to just relax."

Aaron laughed. "Now that sounds like quite a job. My husband, Noel, works for himself. He can do that as well—work intense bursts and then take a bit of time."

"Whereas Aaron here never takes a vacation." The woman at the desk glared at the man who, if my calculations were correct, was her boss.

"Well, there's that. I'm going to Scotland for most of October." He glared back, but the humor soon broke through and he smiled. "Frida's lucky she's such a good employee. Always back talking me."

"Putting you in your place." She glowered, but she had a twinkle in her eye.

I smiled. "I think I'm going to like it here." Honestly, the place had more of a feel of an apartment complex with a busy lobby.

Aaron smiled. "That's the plan. We treat our guests like family. Don't hesitate to ask for whatever you might need, okay? We're also big about privacy, so if you need space, we can offer that too."

"Well, I'm going to get settled and then head to Fifties." I spun my finger around as I tried to orient myself.

He pointed to the door. "Hang a left and it's a block down. Westward."

"Right. I was pretty certain I passed it on my way here. That's close."

"Best burgers in Mission City." Frida grinned. "I do need to see your credit card and driver's license."

"Of course." I pulled my wallet from my back pocket and handed over my ID. As she processed it, I angled myself toward Aaron. "So, you know many people in town?"

He chuckled. "New arrival. I'm American. From California. I fell in love with a visiting Canadian and chased him all the way home." A grin nearly split his face. "I never left."

"Good thing." Frida gestured to the machine.

I inserted my credit card, entered the PIN, and waited for it to make the pretty noise saying I was okay. I would be, of course.

Which hit me with a pang. My money was paying for this, but Erlene's life insurance ensured the kids and I would have fewer worries.

"You okay?" Aaron cocked his head.

"Oh, it's fine. American, eh? You don't have much of an accent."

"I pride myself on having a fairly neutral...accent. Plenty of other places have variations."

"And you're going to Scotland." I tucked my credit card and license back into my wallet and slipped it into my back pocket. "That sounds lovely."

"Delayed honeymoon. We have to go to California in September. Noel's sister, Kendra, is due to give birth. She's perfectly calm. Her husband Javier is losing his mind."

I chuckled. "I'll admit to being very lucky. I have two kids I love desperately, but I got to adopt them and therefore didn't have to be there for the birth."

Aaron smiled. "Noel and I are considering adoption. I might pick your brain...if it's not too personal."

"Nah. Pretty boring story. Well, or not. Their mom was a good friend whom I loved, and she got sick. I married her. Because that's what people do, right? And she was cured and life was great." A pang in my chest. "Until it came back with a vengeance. She was gone within just a couple of months. That was four years ago..." I blinked.

Slowly, telegraphing his movements so I could step away if I wanted, Aaron moved his hand so that, after a moment, it lay on my forearm. "That's rough. No two ways about it."

"Yeah. And, I mean, thank God we married, and I adopted the kids, right? I'm a single dad, but I kind of raised my sisters—who both turned out amazing—so...things worked out."

"They're lucky to have you." He said the words with absolute sincerity.

"I guess. I'm lucky to have them too. Fills a hole in my heart." I wasn't going to tell him about Mom and Nan. I barely knew the dude—no need to dump all my pain on him. "But for sure let's talk about adopting. I can only share what it's like to adopt older kids, though."

"I'll take whatever advice I can get. Would you mind if my, um…" He cocked his head.

"Mind if Noel joins us? Absolutely not. I'm an easygoing guy. Truly." I grinned. "My eldest is at Pride Camp right now. I'm so damn proud of him. He's had a rough go, and I think the wilderness will be good for him. That's why I'm in Mission City. I suppose I could've gone back to Vancouver—it's only an hour's drive—but I want to be close."

"I get that." He offered another smile. "Noel hates being so far from his sister. But she also fell in love with an American. And decided to stay there. I miss my friends, to be sure, but I love my husband so damn much—"

"They're super sappy." Frida pointed her pen. "Which is a joke because Noel was never like that before this guy showed up."

Aaron chortled. "Ah, the joys of small-town living. Wait thirty seconds, and someone will say something that makes it clear how long they've been here."

"And you're mere moments in the grand scheme of things?" I was curious.

"Something like. When I arrived, this place—" He gestured around him at the hotel lobby. "—was a disaster and now it's a stunning masterpiece."

Frida snorted.

Her boss placed a hand across his heart. "You wound me."

She narrowed her eyes. "Well, I wouldn't have stepped foot in the place the way it was, so consider yourself lucky."

"To have the best assistant hotel manager in all of Mission City—" He gazed at her expectantly.

She cleared her throat.

"—Cedar Valley…?"

She shook her head.

"Oh, right. All of British Columbia."

She polished her nametag.

I laughed. "Okay, you two are a hoot." I signed the paper Frida put before me. She handed me a couple of keycards. I nearly turned down the second one, but decided a spare never hurt. I pivoted to Aaron. "Anytime, okay? Just let me know."

"We'll buy you dinner."

"I won't say *no* to that."

"How about White Spot on Tuesday night? Tomorrow is Canada Day, and we're going to be busy. By Tuesday, I'll be ready for a break."

"Sure. Sounds lovely."

"Perfect. I can't wait to tell Noel." He waved as he headed toward a door marked *Private*.

Frida beamed. "I like you."

"The feeling's mutual." I snagged my suitcase and headed for the elevator. A quick ride up to the top floor, and soon I found myself in a scrumptiously appointed room with everything I could possibly need.

After I unpacked, I opened the curtains. Directly below me, just past the street, was a rail yard.

Yay. Good thing I can sleep through anything.

Beyond that, though, was a stunning view of Cedar Valley as well as Mount Baker—the dormant volcano in Washington State.

For just a moment, I considered moving the desk to place it just in front of the window.

You'd sit staring at the view and never get any work done. Alas, that was true. My home office was in a small nook in our condo because, as long as I didn't have any view of any kind, I could focus. Something pretty to look at—even wayward squirrels—and I was liable to get little accomplished.

My stomach rumbled.

I eyed the bed.

Keegan had been up most of the night stressing.

I should've told someone at camp. They might wonder why he's yawning.

Snagging my phone, I debated the best way to deal with the situation.

Call Jai.

Before I could talk myself out of the idea, I searched in my contacts for the number I'd entered when I first received the welcome email.

"Pride Camp. This is Jai Prasad. How may I help you?"

"Hey, Jai, this is Demetrius Fulton. I don't know if you remember me. I'm Keegan's dad."

"I remember. How can I help?"

Is it my imagination, or did his voice just go softer? Does he remember me from all those years ago? "Uh, I forgot to tell you...and Grey...that Keegan was up most of last night stressing. He, uh, didn't get much sleep. He napped on the drive out, but I think that was from exhaustion. If he's a little listless—which happens when he's tired—he might appear bored."

Jai chuckled softly. "He mentioned his crappy night to Grey. He's taking a nap while the other campers settle in. We'll wake him for lunch, which is coming up shortly. Would you like me to call you after lunch and let you know how he's doing?"

No judgement or ridicule over my concern—just a clear understanding.

"That would be amazing. I just..."

"I understand. I've spent a number of years as a counselor—both for LGBTQ kids as well as for special-needs ones. Most parents are protective. How can you not be?"

"I appreciate you understanding. They've just lost so much, and I want him to know I'm here for him. I mean, I'm really hoping he can make it the entire two weeks, but if his stress level is too high, then maybe—"

"Demetrius?"

"Yeah?"

"Why don't we play it by ear? See how each day goes. Keep my number close and call when you need assurances."

"I might need them more than he does."

"That's entirely possible." Jai chuckled. "Are you okay?"

"I'm always okay." Said with more bravado than I felt. Exposing my underbelly with regard to my children? In a heartbeat. For anything else? No. I had to be the strong one.

"All right. Have a good afternoon, Demetrius."

I liked the sound of my name off his lips. "I'm having lunch at Fifties."

"Best burgers in Mission City."

"That's the rumor. Uh, thank you."

"You're most welcome."

I didn't want to hang up. I wanted to keep talking to him. To make him laugh. To see if I could tease him the way I used to.

But I wouldn't. He was working—I needed to respect that.

"Thanks again."

"My pleasure."

In the end, I disconnected.

Chapter Three

Jai

I stared at my cell phone for an extra-long time.

That voice. I'd never met the man, so I didn't understand why his voice sounded so familiar.

Still, I searched my memory. Not anyone I'd known growing up in Mission City. Although I didn't know his age, he was obviously older than me. So that knocked off university unless he was a mature student—but I'd known everyone in my analytics program.

Not the accounting firm. I'd been the only person of color there—which still, six years on, rankled.

Obviously not from the time I'd spent at the camp in Nova Scotia.

Demetrius Fulton was just too...distinctive. Noticeable.

And yet...

I pushed the elusive memory out of my mind. I'd returned to my office to send a quick update email to Alessandra to let her know all the campers had arrived. We had five who were male-identifying, four female, and one nonbinary. I worried they'd be in a cabin by themselves, but Chris said they were fine in the female dormitory.

None of the parents had fussed about it. As far as I could tell, every parent who had enrolled their child into our program was...accepting. Which made sense.

And the campers were more teenagers than kids. The ages ranged from twelve to fourteen.

In a few weeks, we had an older cohort coming. And then possibly expanding to add a camp for kids whose siblings were LGBTQ. They needed special time as well.

Alessandra's responding email caught my notice. She, along with Smith, would join us for lunch.

Which was now upon us.

I grabbed my baseball cap and headed out. I'd worn a button-down shirt and chinos for the arrival of the campers with their parents. Now I wore blue jeans, a T-shirt, and the ball cap. The afternoon promised to be hot, and I might change again, into khaki shorts.

Upon entering the great room, where one corner was set aside for eating, I did a quick headcount.

Keegan wasn't here.

Neither was Cody.

Makenna was encouraging the teens to grab trays and head over to the buffet while Grey headed my way.

I nodded a greeting.

He returned the gesture. "Cody's getting Keegan. We didn't want him sleeping too long, but Cody will decide what's the best course of action."

"Clearly Keegan's nervous." We were well beyond the hearing range of the other kids.

"He is. So's Paisley. She keeps pulling at her hair. Her mom warned Cody about that."

And it had been on her intake form. As a child, she'd pulled out so much hair she'd had a bald spot.

"You'll all keep an eye on her?"

"Yep. We're going to focus on distraction. She's expressed an interest in art, and we've got lots of that planned."

Cody's studies included art-therapy classes, and he hoped to put that experience to good use.

"Oh, there they are." Grey focused on the new arrivals.

Keegan's hands were deep in his pockets, and he was staring at the floor. Still, anything that got him out of his dorm room could be considered a win. He was so petite compared to Cody who was clearly trying not to overwhelm him. The guy was just big...something I hoped would seem more comforting than intimidating.

My phone buzzed in my pocket. To Grey, I said, "Let me know if you need anything."

He nodded. "You bet." And then he was off.

I retrieved my phone. Alessandra had texted that they'd arrived, so I headed out to greet them.

Alessandra and Smith MacLean were a study in contrasts. She was short, petite, and had a riot of long, black, curly hair.

He was tall, broad, and with fine blond hair.

Alessandra spotted me and waved.

I hustled over. "So glad you're here."

She grinned. "Hopefully not because there's a problem already."

"No, of course not. All the campers are here and settling in. As far as I can tell, Makenna and Grey have everything under control."

"And Cody?" Smith adjusted his sunglasses, making me aware I wasn't wearing mine.

"Helping Keegan."

Alessandra nodded. "I think he'll need extra TLC." She had access to the files as well, given her counseling background, and she was considered an unpaid consultant.

Smith didn't have that privilege.

We tried to keep exposure to the confidential files to a minimum. The only offsite person who could access them was Dr. Kennedy Dixon—and that was so if Cody needed backup, she could familiarize herself. I doubted he'd need to speak to his mentor...but the option existed.

"Would you like to come and meet the kids?" I winced. "Campers. I have to stop thinking of them as *kids*."

"Because they're closer in age to you than you are to me." Smith grinned.

Alessandra poked him in the ribs. "Not quite." She squinted. "Oh God, they are." She pivoted to her husband. "Does that make you old or them super young?"

"Or just plop me in the middle." I spoke up, hoping to try to avoid a fight. They'd never argued before, but I hadn't spent much time in their presence.

Smith laughed. "We've left Tarah alone with Wesley."

Alessandra glared. "Nice try. My friend is perfectly capable of caring for my child. I'm allowed to leave him alone once in a while."

Their son was about twenty months old.

"You could've brought him. Just about everyone likes toddlers." The little tyke intimidated me, but that was because I had little exposure to young children. No siblings and no cousins who came around anymore. Few deep friendships, either. Except my best friend from school, Arnav. Most of my life over the last six years had been consumed with camps, so forming bonds outside of that environment proved difficult. Before that…? I didn't like to think about it.

"You know, we might consider doing that. I want him to be exposed to more people." Alessandra grinned. "We take him out, but not in an environment like this. He's going through a clingy phase. Being with Tarah helps, but he needs more time around new people on his own terms."

"He'll always be welcome here. Now, are you interested in some roast chicken with green beans, mashed potatoes, and fresh-baked buns?"

"Given breakfast was six hours ago? You better believe it." Alessandra grabbed Smith's hand and directed him to follow her to the great hall.

I took a place beside him. "Things are going well."

"I'm glad to hear it. The municipal forestry people are due to visit tomorrow. They just want to make certain the paths are clear and ready to be used."

"Makenna and Grey hiked them yesterday."

"True. Don't mind Dean—he's a stickler. He also probably wants to review campfire rules and all things forest."

"He's the guy…" I wracked my brain.

"Australian," Smith supplied. "Super cute and very taken."

"And not your type anyway." Alessandra opened the door and gazed up at her husband.

"Right. Raven-haired beauties with dark-brown soulful eyes and the ability to put me in my place with just a glare are." He smiled at me. "And Dean is also super married."

"Oh?" None of this had come up in my conversation with the blond man who had stunning blue eyes and a knowledge of trees I could never rival. What did I know? Don't light a match. We'd had dry conditions for a while now—April's showers long forgotten and June being just one long furnace of dry heat.

"To Adam, another great Mission City guy." Smith removed his sunglasses as we stepped inside and then tucked them into the front of his cotton button-down shirt. It was actually open several buttons, and he wasn't wearing a tie.

"Dean and Adam." I didn't know either of them. Or I didn't think I did. My time in Mission City ended more than a decade ago. I'd gone to stay in Vancouver to attend the University of British Columbia. Then I'd found a place to live in the city—with *him*—and I'd never come home for holidays. Even though Mission City was just an hour east of Vancouver. I hadn't felt the need to revisit my unhappy childhood. Then I shoved all thoughts of my ex deep down where I wouldn't have to deal with that thought either.

So why did you come home? And when are you going to tell your parents?

My parents probably still believed I was back in Nova Scotia. Or I assumed that was what they thought. We hadn't spoken in a very long time. I was the disappointment. Even if my ex hadn't shared *everything*, my parents still hadn't approved of me. No matter what I did, it wasn't good enough. Even studying finance to follow in the family tradition didn't meet their approval. I had been groomed to take over the management of their extensive holdings.

Instead I'd wound up as a camp counselor for queer teens on the other side of the country.

But you're home now. You might run into them...

Not likely. They didn't shop at the grocery store or pick up their prescriptions—they had *staff* for that.

"Jai?" Alessandra gazed up at me.

Not so far to look. I was closer in height to her than Smith.

"All good. Just reviewing some budget things in my mind." Even as the words came out, I inwardly winced.

"If you need more money, you let me know." Smith held my gaze with his compelling and oddly colored eyes.

Alessandra said they were azure.

I'd never seen anyone else with that eye color.

"We're good. I think being fiscally prudent is a good thing, and I'm still sure the campers will want for nothing."

"You'll do your best, which is all we can ask." Alessandra shot a glare at her husband. "Money doesn't always solve every problem."

"Says you." He smirked.

"If you gave it all away, we wouldn't have any for our son." She arched an eyebrow.

"Kid has to make his own way in the world. I smell barbecue chicken." He headed toward the buffet.

Alessandra laughed. "I'm the one who's going to have to make sure Wesley doesn't get spoiled." She grinned. Then her expression sobered. "Two things."

I nodded.

"Ask for money if you need it. He teeters between multi-millionaire and billionaire—and will never admit it—and I trust your discretion."

"Absolutely." I'd been aware they had money, and they didn't flaunt it. Not that kind of wealth, though—that even dwarfed my family's *old money*.

"Great. I want to meet the campers."

"Wait."

She cocked her head.

"You said, two things…"

"Oh right." Her face lit. "For fuck's sake, Jai, have fun."

Chapter Four

Demetrius

The smells of a diner assailed me as I stepped into Fifties—frying meat, French fries, and...eau de ketchup? Whatever. I'd found my happy place.

"Hey, welcome to Fifties." A bubbly blonde with beautiful blue eyes beamed. "Just you?"

"Yeah."

She glanced around. "Uh..."

Every booth in the place was full. As was every stool at the counter.

"I don't mind waiting."

"Or he can join us. If he's amenable, that is." A strong voice came from behind me.

I pivoted to find a South Asian man sitting with a Black man in the closest booth.

The first guy patted the seat next to him. "I'm Arnav. This is my husband Foster. We were just commenting on how we hadn't met anyone new recently."

Foster rolled his eyes. But a shy smile lit his face.

I judged him to be about my age or maybe a couple of years older. I'd wondered how many other Black folks I might meet while in Mission City. The apparent immediate answer was two—previously Aaron and now Foster.

And Foster was gay as well. And married to a cute guy.

"You're sure?"

"He wouldn't have invited you if he wasn't sure." Foster spoke quietly, but with some strength behind the words. "We're friendly."

I grinned. "Cool." I turned to the server, but she was already at the back of the restaurant dealing with something. I eased into the booth.

"We can flag Sarabeth to get you a menu." Foster glanced behind him, toward the counter. "Or I might be able to—"

"Fifties has the best burgers in Mission City, right?" My smile didn't falter.

"Well, best in Cedar Valley." Arnav beamed. "Those would be very good words."

"I like White Spot as well." Foster leaned forward conspiratorially. "But don't tell Sarabeth."

"I've had White Spot. They make delicious burgers. But we have White Spots in Vancouver. We do not have a Fifties." I frowned. "That I know of."

"Nope." Arnav popped his *p*. "One of a kind. No franchise. So you're from Vancouver?"

"I apologize." Sarabeth magically appeared. "Do you need a menu?"

"No, I'm good. I'll have a cheeseburger."

"Great. And to drink?"

"Uh—"

"Do you like milkshakes?" Foster met my gaze.

I nodded.

"Ever have a blueberry milkshake?"

I shook my head.

"You're in for a treat." His soft brown eyes radiated amusement.

"Okay, Sarabeth. Blueberry milkshake, cheeseburger, and extra fries."

"Brilliant. We're busy, but I'll see if the chef can make yours with theirs." She pointed between Arnav and Foster.

"No rush. I'm not in a hurry. In fact, I've got all day." I glanced around. "But I won't hold up the table."

She smiled. "I think I like you." Then she was gone.

"Okay." I gazed back and forth between Arnav and Foster. "You just randomly invite strangers to your table?"

Foster giggled.

Yes, giggled.

So at odds with the forty-something man before me.

Arnav wagged his finger. But his grin was just as wide.

"We had our second date here. And we've run into friends over the months we've been coming here."

"Not to be too bold..." Foster ducked his head for a moment, then met my gaze. "You seemed like a nice person."

"Uh..."

"Your smile." Arnav shrugged. "We had a ten-second silent conversation and then we invited you. Perhaps impetuous."

"Except our friend Ravi invited a stranger to join him along with his husband. And they wound up helping that stranger find a place to live with another friend of theirs—who wound marrying the stranger. By then, voilà, they all became friends, and then we met them, and they became our friends..." Foster shrugged.

"So, lots of friendly people in this small town?"

"Yep." He beamed.

"Apparently lots of friendly gay guys." My head spun at his explanation, but I'd sort of figured out two gay couples.

For just a moment, Foster stilled.

I added, "I'm bi." Because that seemed like the right thing to say and because I probably wouldn't have sat here if I was homophobic or going to throw shade on gay people.

"Okay." Foster ducked his head again. "Ravi and Maddox are married. That stranger, Dean, is married to Adam. Our friends Everett and Rayne just got married."

"Rayne being a guy." Arnav grinned. "And a bit of a..."

"Friendly." Foster supplied that quickly.

I was supercurious what Arnav had been about to say.

"One blueberry milkshake." Delivered with a grin, a straw, and a long spoon. Sarabeth nodded, then headed down toward the back of the diner.

"Is it always this busy?" I removed the wrapper from the straw.

"Saturdays generally are." Arnav wrinkled his nose. "But with Canada Day tomorrow, there are likely tourists in town."

"Mission City doesn't have a huge tourism industry." Foster nodded toward my milkshake as if to encourage me. "I work in construction. Always need more houses. We're at the end of the commuter railway line, and although prices are expensive, they're the cheapest around."

"I don't know much about real estate. I have a condo in Vancouver. Tight quarters with a teen and a pre-teen."

"You're a dad?" Arnav grinned. "That's amazing. We've registered to become foster parents and are waiting. I mean, you never hope a kid needs a place to live—but we've got one in case they do."

"Big house with a dog and a backyard." Foster said the words almost as if he felt he had to convince me.

"I love my kids."

"Are they with you? I mean, not *here* obviously." Foster winced.

I smiled. "Alaina's doing some hiking over on Vancouver Island." I considered my next words carefully. "My son, Keegan, is attending Pride Camp."

"How old?" Arnav scratched his nose.

"Thirteen."

"Rough age. No matter what."

"I know. And I thought kids were...more accepting. Unfortunately, Keegan's been picked on by a group of older kids—"

"Bullies?" Arnav held my gaze with concerned dark-brown eyes.

"Yeah."

"Ouch."

"Right? So I've considered pulling him out of that school and sending him somewhere else. Or even picking up stakes and leaving. The neighborhood isn't the best, and maybe a fresh start..." I contemplated my drink. "But does that give him the message that it's okay to run away from your problems?"

"Sometimes it is." Foster spoke quietly.

I met his gaze.

"I don't tend to tell folks this often. But something tells me you might need to hear it. I was in an emotionally abusive relationship for almost ten years. Maybe if someone had taught me that it's okay to walk away, I might have. I had a rough childhood, and I thought I'd found someone to take care of me. That ended disastrously, and I didn't think I'd ever pick up the pieces." He reached for Arnav's hand. "Yet, I did. And, eventually, I met this handsome man."

Arnav chuckled.

"I gave love another shot. Put my heart on the line. That wasn't easy."

"So you're saying it's okay for us to try something new?" I considered his words. And how hard it must've been for him to be honest with me.

"I'm saying that although the unknown can be scary—especially for a kid—staying where you're miserable and being bullied isn't an answer either."

"Thanks. We'll see how things work out at Pride Camp. They've got such an amazing staff. Cody, Grey, Makenna, and Jai—"

"Jai?" Arnav perked.

"Got your food." Sarabeth arrived with a tray of the most heavenly smelling grub.

We thanked her profusely before she headed away.

I sipped my milkshake, waiting for my burger to cool just a smidge.

"Jai, you say?" Arnav clearly was picking up where we left off. He poked his French toast with a fork and then dumped a lake of syrup on it.

"Yes. Do you know him?"

"Well, my friend from childhood was Jai Prasad. He moved away years ago. I hadn't heard he was back. We lost touch..." He snagged a piece of bacon. "So even if it's not the same guy, I should really find my Jai and touch base with him." He bit into the bacon.

I poured some ketchup on my plate and dunked a fry. What were the odds the name was identical? "About thirty? Slender? Kind of looks like you?" Because that wasn't rude...right?

Arnav laughed. "Yeah, lots of Indian guys named Jai. He was shorter than me, but that doesn't mean anything. Plenty of young men get taller. He did head off to UBC. He was, I think, doing a business degree. I studied law." He contemplated his bacon. "He was my friend despite the fact I was out and proud. Not a lot of kids were back then. Seventeen years is a long time and yeah, I'd hoped things were changing. I'm sorry your son is going through that."

"Pride Camp sounds like the right place for him." Foster hesitated, fork poised over his meatloaf. "Him? I hate to make assumptions."

"Keegan goes by he/him. We had that discussion, and I made it clear we live in a judgement-free household. He's said, at least for now, he identifies that way. The camp has a group of teenagers from a variety of backgrounds. I have my phone close, even though I know he's safe."

"Does Pride Camp have a website? Might Jai's photo be on it? Or some other social media?" Arnav took a bite of his syrup-drenched French toast.

Inwardly, I smiled. "Uh, his photo isn't on the website. I don't think the camp has social media—might attract unwanted attention."

"True that." Foster cut another piece. "Not everyone is accepting around here. We still get looks sometimes."

"Like by Jai's parents." Arnav poked his food again. "You remember? That benefit we went to?"

"Oh, that couple? The ones Samara put in their place when they made that comment?" Foster met my gaze. "Samara is Arnav's protective older sister—"

"—one of six—"

"Eldest of six," Foster continued smoothly, all the while grinning. "And this older couple were going on about how gay couples shouldn't be allowed to have children."

Arnav grunted.

"Right? Whether she realized Arnav and I were together, I can't be certain. Or if she was just spouting off."

Another grunt.

"Before either of us could speak, Samara launched into a litany about all the straight couples who abused their children."

"Did she know this couple?" I dipped another fry in ketchup, popped it into my mouth, then eyed my burger.

"I don't think so. I can honestly say that wouldn't have made any difference to Samara. She'll tell anyone off—especially if she thinks they're discriminating or hurting other people." Foster dipped his meatloaf in the thick gravy. "So they were your friend's parents. I didn't realize."

"If he'd ever come out as gay, there would've been hell to pay. They knew I was out back then." He poised his fork in the air. "Which means they probably figured out you and I were together—matching weddings bands and all—and made the comment anyway."

"Likely because of us." Foster ate the slice and moaned in bliss.

I picked up my burger. "So if Jai was gay...?" I bit, letting the succulent juices hit my tongue.

"Today? I'd like to think he'd be able to stand up to them. Back then? No way. They held way too much power over him. He got a scholarship, but the Sauder School of Business at UBC is damn expensive. He lived on campus—partly to get away from them. We...drifted apart. I regret that."

I swallowed the delicious mouthful. "I suppose you could call the camp and see if he's the same guy." Because I certainly wasn't going to out the man—if he was gay. Or explain where I knew him from before. Likely, given the timing, it had been just after he finished university when we'd encountered each other.

Although I had zero doubt the guy was my pup friend, he didn't appear to remember me. I had no idea how to remind him.

Or, conversely, if he remembered and was just putting on a good act, did I have the right to approach him?

I just didn't know.

Arnav snagged his second piece of bacon. "I'll give him a shout. I'd rather go down there, but I don't want to spook anyone, and if he's not my friend, then it would look super weird."

"Sounds sensible." I bit into my burger.

"And how are things here?"

Naturally, Sarabeth managed to arrive while all three of us had food in our mouths.

We all gave her a thumbs-up.

An hour later, with a slice of lemon merengue pie in a to-go box—and an invitation to join Arnav and Foster on Monday night—I headed back to the hotel.

Chapter Five

Jai

"Pride Camp, this is Jai." I squinted at my laptop, debated getting up to close the blinds so the sunlight wasn't hitting the screen at a bad angle, and then decided being able to see outside was more important.

"Jai...Prasad...?"

My skin prickled. Coming back to Mission City had always been a risk. In that instant, it didn't feel worth it. I cleared my throat. "Yes. May I ask who I'm speaking to?"

"It's Arnav!"

No missing the excitement.

"Arnav Mehta."

I blinked. "Arnav?" I only knew one Arnav and his last name was Mehta. "How are you?"

"I was going to ask you that question. Like, *how the hell are you*? As opposed to *why the hell didn't you tell me you were back in town?*"

A question he essentially just asked.

"I'm good. Busy, but good. I've only been in town for two months."
I both winced and held my breath.

"Right. Well, summer camp would keep you busy. I'm just surprised I didn't know." With just the slightest tinge of hurt.

"I haven't really told anyone. I wanted to get settled first, you know?
My focus has been on the campers. This is our first year in operation,
so plenty of kinks to work out." *Really? I just used the word* kinks *for fuck's sake.*

"Understandable. And I haven't spotted you—but then I wasn't
looking either. Back then...we drifted... My bad, really. I was so focused
on law school, and I just wasn't paying attention, and then one day
I realized we hadn't spoken in a while and I tried calling, and your
number was disconnected. I seemed to recall you'd gotten a job with a
big finance company, but I couldn't remember which one—"

"All good." Because I wasn't going to explain the weird journey
my life had taken. Or what had me turning tail and running from
Vancouver. From British Columbia. To the other side of the country.
But I could provide an explanation for my return. "Pride Camp was
hiring a new director, and I figured I could put my finance degree to
good use."

"Yeah, they're lucky to have you. I can barely add."

A bit of an exaggeration—but math hadn't been Arnav's strength.
No, his ability to smooth talk anyone had been his gift. I'd always
thought salesperson would've been an exceptional backup career if this
law thing didn't work out. "How's lawyering?"

"Good. Keeping me out of trouble. Hey, I saw your parents last
month. They didn't say anything about you coming home. Of course
they were too busy putting down gay people. You know before I could
even say anything, Samara was right there, standing up for her baby
brother and his husband."

"I remember Samara, and wait—" I rubbed my forehead. "Did you just say you're married?" I wasn't even going to try to explain why my parents hadn't said anything to him. Something about me being dead to them. If they knew I was running Pride Camp, they'd lose their ever-loving shit.

Arnav chuckled. "Yep. Almost six months. Go figure, right? An older man, at that. A gorgeous, sexy, slightly older man who's glaring at me right now."

Slightly older? I wasn't going to ask. And somehow I'd envisioned him alone as we spoke. I hadn't said anything I was uncomfortable with, but I found the idea of him having someone there listening vaguely disconcerting.

"Oh, sorry, I should've mentioned Foster before now. Look, why don't you come over? Say Monday night?"

"The camp..."

"You don't get a night off? We can make it another—"

"It's fine. Actually, I'm only here for emergencies at night. I live on the property. But one night away will be fine."

"Great. I have a new house. Yes, I finally moved out of my parents' basement."

A distinctive chuckle quietly reverberated through the phone.

"Oh hush, you." Arnav again laughed. "Foster's one to watch. He comes across all quiet and shy, but beware. Once he knows you, he's got a wicked sense of humor."

"Really?" I didn't know a *Foster*.

"Yes. So consider yourself warned. Can I text you my address to this number? Or do you want to write it down? Oh, or I can send an email—"

"Text is fine." This time, I chuckled. Arnav always had a lot to say. And had to say it quickly, given how many sisters he had.

I'd spent a lot of my youth in that house.

A pang for having left my friend behind resonated in my chest.

You could've told him. He would've understood. He wouldn't have judged.

All things that were very true. And water under the bridge at this point. Still... "Uh, Arnav?"

"Yeah?"

"I'm gay."

"Uh, Jai?"

"Yeah."

A long pause. "I want to say I figured because you're the director of Pride Camp—although we both know any qualified person could do the job."

"True."

"But I've sort of mostly and yeah kind of known since you were about fifteen."

My stomach plummeted.

"I never said anything. I didn't figure it was my place. And you didn't do anything specific..." He cleared his throat. "Foster is amazed at my inarticulateness."

I still held my breath.

"I wasn't attracted to you. And you were clearly, firmly in the closet. And I also might've been wrong. I wasn't willing to screw up a friendship. I hoped, if you ever came out, that you'd feel comfortable telling me."

"Yeah."

"And you just have, so we're good. Right?"

"Yeah." *See how simple that was? You could've done it fourteen years ago and saved yourself the heartache.* Except if I'd come out in high school, there would've been hell to pay. When my secrets had been revealed, the shitstorm I'd expected had materialized. Only it had been so very much worse than I expected. "Thank you."

"No problem. Oh, we have a friend coming over as well. I hope that's okay."

"Of course." Even as I said the words, though, I longed to pull them back. Truly, I couldn't think of a single person I wanted to see. Well, his sisters would be okay, but he'd said *friend* and not *family*. "What can I bring?"

"Yourself. Oh, and be prepared for puppies." With that, he cut the line.

Dogs?

Oh God, does he know?

Breathe.

Who would've told him? And if he did know—because of some painful quirk of the universe—wouldn't he have said something?

Again, I reminded myself to breathe.

Not so easy to do.

I logged out of the system, shut my laptop, and gazed out the window.

Grey and Makenna were down by the water with the campers. The plan was to do some canoeing tomorrow.

Cody sat on a picnic table with his feet on the seat. His arms were spread behind him, and he had his body pointed to the sun. The guy had fair coloring and so always applied SPF 60.

You could join him. Enjoy a moment's quiet before dinner.

I planned to eat dinner with the group tonight, but then aimed to generally make myself scarce at night from now on. Everyone knew where to find me.

My phone buzzed with an incoming text.

An address and a photo of two adorable-looking dogs. Both actual pooches and neither was of a breed I recognized. Possibly mutts?

Shot back a thumbs-up and tucked my phone into my back pocket. I grabbed my sunglasses and ball cap and headed out.

I tried to be quiet, but Cody clearly heard my feet on the gravel as he sat up straighter and turned his head in my direction. "You going to join me?"

"Sure." *Casual. Like this wasn't always the plan.* I sat on the table with him. "I won't ask how it's going..."

He chuckled. "Nothing to report. I have no idea, at this point, how much I'm going to be useful."

"You've got times set aside for each camper, right?"

"Yep. Every couple of days. We've let them know there's nothing wrong with wanting more and it's also okay if they feel they need less."

"Yeah?"

"Brielle, Francis, and Elliott all come across as really settled and content. We both know first impressions might be misleading." Cody scratched his nose.

"True." I considered. "And you're worried about?"

"Keegan for sure. The young man has some kind of underlying issues. Even putting aside the fact he's an orphan—his word, not mine." His file painted a bleak picture of a kid in pain.

"You met his stepfather." *The memorable guy.*

"Mr. Fulton? Seems like a nice guy. Keegan had good things to say. About the gentleman stepping up when his mom got sick, marrying her, and then adopting him and his sister."

"That's a lot."

"There *are* good people in the world. I would definitely put Chris's parents in that category."

"Yeah?"

Cody nodded. "Chris says their parents are completely supportive. Excited, even. Well, of their child feeling comfortable enough to attend camp. High school next year is a whole other thing."

"They're from West Vancouver, right?"

"Yeah. Very conservative area. Their parents are worried about how they'll do in high school."

"Well, we'll do our best to see they're prepared, right?" I slanted a glance at Cody.

"I counseled several nonbinary teens during my practicum. Each kid is unique, though. All four of Chris's grandparents insist on gendering them."

"Ouch." Of course if I'd been nonbinary or trans, my parents would've done the same damn thing.

"Yeah. So all the aunts, uncles, and cousins feel free to do the same. Chris is hanging in there, but it's not easy on them."

"I'd say not. I was reviewing the applicants for the next session. Two trans teenagers."

"Just as tough."

I nodded. "Both have parental consent to attend, and sometimes that's the highest hurdle."

"This would be the session at the end of July?"

"Yes. Looks like a good group of kids. Sorry, teens." This next group were fifteen- to seventeen-year-olds.

"There's plenty of space for more teens." Cody sniffed. "Dinner smells amazing."

"The camp is designed to hold twenty-four campers. I worried we might have problems if we waited until the last minute, but that doesn't appear to be the case."

"Part of that is the tough economy. Not as many jobs for teenagers."

"True." And LGBTQ kids tended to have higher unemployment rates. Which just sucked.

"And I'm sure some is because of the special nature of what you're doing."

"That's also entirely possible. Twenty-four would be almost impossible for you to manage."

He shrugged. "If we have campers with serious issues needing major interventions? Yes. Alessandra's offered to step up. She loves being a mother, but she's also got that *must be helping people all the time* gene."

"I believe you have the same one."

He burst out laughing. "Oh, that's so true. Kennedy recognized it in me immediately and was happy to direct my interest toward counseling and the PhD program at Simon Fraser University. I just thought..." He cleared his throat. "I knew I could be gay. I knew I could be a psychologist. I knew there were gay psychologists...."

"You just hadn't pieced it together for yourself."

"Right. During my undergrad, I met Justin Bridges—a gay counselor. One of Kennedy's other successful mentees. He's amazing at his job."

"Did she say he's pursuing a PhD?" I seemed to recall that coming up in conversation.

Cody chuckled. "He tells me he looks up to me because I actually had the guts to do the program."

"Oh?"

"It's not cheap. I think that was one of the reasons he told himself he couldn't do it. I'm not speaking out of turn when I say he lacked confidence. As I progressed through my studies, he came to see he could do it as well. He's just finished another year. Pretty soon, Kennedy and Denise won't be the only psychologists at the ranch."

Dr. Denise Lang was a psychologist who specialized in counseling children in trauma.

"Kennedy attracts the best."

"That she does."

"She trying to get you to sign on?"

Cody shot me a glance.

I shrugged. "I would, if I were her. And as much as I love Pride Camp, we only operate during the summer. As long as she's willing to let you come back every summer—for as long as you want—I think you should go for it. Unless working for your mentor would be stifling."

"Oh God, working for her would be the opposite of that. She's brilliant, Jai. And I'm not just saying that..." He waved his hand around. "She took care of me when I was at my most vulnerable. Then turned that empathy into a kick in the pants. She knocked me right out of my apathy and onto the path I've chosen."

"Well, we're glad you found your calling." I waved in response to Makenna's gesture. "Dinner?"

"Hell yeah, I'm starving."

Despite my stomach being in knots for most of the day—with worry about whether or not we could pull this off—I was as well.

Chapter Six

Demetrius

"**N**o problems finding the place?" Foster offered a broad smile when he opened the front door Monday night.

"Not at all. Glad you didn't set the time earlier, though. Some yahoos were setting off firecrackers half the night. I hadn't thought to bring earplugs—which would be helpful with the trains as well. This seems counterintuitive, but apparently downtown Mission City can be a noisy place."

Foster laughed. "Especially the corner where the Grand Hotel is located. That's a major intersection—and there are few of those." He gestured for me to follow him in. "I'm also from Vancouver and accustomed to more noise. Up here, where we're near the end of a dead-end street? Barely a whisper."

As if on cue, two dogs came tearing into the foyer, yapping like crazy.

My host slammed the door. "Queenie!"

The smaller dog's jaw snapped shut.

"Good girl." Foster pivoted his attention. "Taffy." Less bite and more...pleading?

She eyed him before finally closing her mouth as well.

"You're such good girls." He cooed that, producing some kind of bacon-resembling thing from his pocket. He broke off two pieces. "Sit."

Both dogs plopped onto their butts.

"Down."

Again—compliance.

"Good girls." He gave them each a piece.

Taffy licked her chops and then headed back from where she'd come.

Queenie continued to stare.

Foster held out his hands. "Nothing."

She eyed the pocket where he'd tucked the rest of the treat.

He shook his head.

After what felt like forever, she eyed me for a moment, then headed toward the back of the house.

"Did your dog just shrug?"

"As in *I had to try?* Yep, that's Queenie. All rescue and all attitude."

"She's adorable." I didn't just love human pups.

"She's a handful. We got her as soon as we moved in. I always wanted a dog as a kid. As did Arnav. Next, we're hoping to be blessed with foster kids. Or adopting. We just want to help kids in need. I know what it's like. Being a foster kid," he clarified.

I held up the fruit tray I'd brought because I wasn't certain how to react to that level of pain—even if transitory.

His face lit. "Blueberries!"

"And cherries, watermelon, as well as strawberries. No cantaloupe. That stuff's nasty."

Dark-brown eyes flashed amusement. "Don't tell Arnav that."

I mimed zipping my lips.

"Come through to the back. Fortunately the bugs aren't too bad yet. Near the end of the season, it can get nasty."

"How long have you had the house?"

The sand-colored two-story brick house resembled the others on the street. Kind of like Nan's house back in East Van. I'd been sorry to sell it, but I'd needed the money to pay for Imani's and Malaya's educations. No bank would give a twenty-one-year-old, who was supporting his eighteen-year-old twin sisters, a mortgage. Even if the property was paid off. And I'd been forced to sell during a downturn in the economy. Today that house was worth five times what I sold it for nearly twenty years ago.

Yeah...that still stung.

But Imani was a forensic pathologist for the Royal Canadian Mounted Police, and Malaya was an urban planner for the City of Langley. Both important jobs that required serious amounts of education.

Which I'd been happy to pay for. They'd graduated debt-free and were able to start their new lives, far away from East Van.

Imani lived in a condo in the west end of Vancouver, while Malaya, her engineering husband, and their two sons, lived on a farm near Langley. My sister was not a farmer. At all. Instead, they leased their blueberry fields to a local grower. Along with the extra income, they got free berries for about a month a year.

"We've been in the house about six months." Foster put the tray on the counter.

I pulled my thoughts back to the present.

"I'm going to let you in on a little secret—Arnav and I haven't been together that long. We met and..." He interlaced his fingers.

"Ah."

"I'd given up looking. I considered myself washed up—"

"Hey." I frowned.

He wagged his finger at me. "I *considered* myself. I'd been out of an abusive relationship for almost five years, but I still hadn't come out. I rented a nice place in Mission City, but I didn't have deep roots here. Hell, I didn't feel like I belonged anywhere—except the construction sites. The company I work for focuses on low-income housing. I got a sense of satisfaction from that, at least." He opened the fridge. "Cola, diet cola, ginger ale, fizzy orange, root beer, or an actual beer?"

"Not a drinker." I put the fruit tray on the kitchen island.

"Neither are we."

"But you have a sweet tooth." I had to tease.

"We have so many nieces and nephews I can't keep track—all Arnav's. He loves to send them home high on sugar. Somehow thinking his sisters will never send their children back."

"And they continue to?"

He offered me a wide grin. "Funny that—free babysitting."

"Orange fizzy sounds great—I haven't had one of those in ages."

"They're nice. One of Beena's girls likes them. And..." He squinted. "One of Minal's boys."

"How *do* you keep them straight?"

He gestured to a drawer. "I have a notebook. A very full notebook." He offered a hint of a smile. "I want to be the best uncle ever."

I cocked my head. "I'm sure you are."

"How do you know?" He didn't appear offended...just truly curious.

"Instinct. I mean, anyone who keeps a book with notes about someone else's kids is pretty damn special."

"That's what I keep telling him." Arnav opened the screen door and stepped inside. He removed his sunglasses. "Glad you're here."

I pointed to the fruit tray. "No cantaloupe."

His face fell.

Foster laughed his ass off.

I sipped my fizzy orange drink, hiding a smile.

"Just see if I give you the prime cut of beef." Arnav jutted his chin.

Foster slung an arm around his waist and placed a kiss to his husband's temple. "Be nice."

"I'm always nice."

The doorbell rang.

The two dogs, who had been snoozing on respective beds, leapt up, started barking their heads off, and tore off toward the front of the house.

Arnav pointed at Foster. "You're the bad influence."

"You're really going to try that with me?" He grinned. "I blame Taffy." He turned to me. "My neighbor is on her honeymoon with her new bride. As a gift, we offered to watch the holy terror."

"Hey." Arnav called over his shoulder as he walked down the hall. "Taffy is a sweetheart. Aren't you, darling? Now, can you please stop barking?" All said in a very sing-songy voice.

"Queenie? Taffy? Treats." Foster winked.

Nails clacked on the hardwood floor as the two dogs raced into the kitchen. Both dogs dropped to their butts.

Foster removed the jerky, split it in two, and eyed them.

They vibrated with excitement.

"It's just this way." Arnav's voice carried.

Foster gave each dog her treat.

"Oh." A startled exclamation had me turning.

And facing Jai.

Who appeared stunned.

"You two know each other, right?" Arnav moved to the fridge. "You still like root beer?"

"You remembered? Uh, yeah. Thanks." Still Jai held my gaze.

"We should've probably told you Demetrius would be here." Foster took the can from his husband and poured the drink into a glass. "Sorry, I wasn't thinking. You don't have some kind of conflict of interest or something, do you?"

"They're not dating." Arnav snagged a strawberry.

"It's, uh, fine." Jai shook his head.

But didn't look the least bit at ease.

"I'm Foster." The man stuck out his hand.

Jai shook it.

"I'm looking forward to hearing about all the shit my husband got into during his misspent youth."

"Hey. My sisters have shared all." Arnav gazed at me. "Seriously. Six sisters. Zero secrets."

Slowly, Jai smiled. "I can think of a few—"

"Oh no, you don't. We're heading out to the barbecue. I have chicken marinating. Grab a strawberry."

Jai complied and let himself be ushered out the back door.

"We can join them." Foster offered a smile. "I told Arnav surprising each of you wasn't a good idea."

I waved him off. "No worries on my end. Jai sent me a report this morning. My son's struggling, but did some canoeing yesterday. At least the boy knows how to swim. His mom was good about preparing them for life."

"But not you?" He cocked his head.

"What? Oh, right. I didn't get involved with the kids until they were five and three. Just an honorary uncle at first. Then I married their mom." I shrugged. "Then she passed."

"I'm so sorry. Must've been really tough, raising kids on your own."

"Yeah, had its moments. Especially when some fine folk saw me out with two little white kids."

"I get that." He winced. "Mission City is still primarily white folk. The East Asian population is next in size with Indigenous after that. Not so many Black people, although that's changing. I've met a bunch of people in my time here. My dentist is Black. The harbormaster is. The arborist my company contracts. Two lawyers Arnav is forever fighting in court..." He grinned. "And others as well." He scrunched his nose. "And most of the guys I just mentioned are gay and married."

"And all from Mission City?"

"Not one of the lawyers. Oh, nor the harbormaster. I'm not, as I said. Despite Cedar Valley being very conservative—and very religious—I've encountered plenty of accepting people. *Live and let live.*"

"That's great. I'll admit I was surprised to find Pride Camp in Cedar Valley. But I read about the founders, and they sound like great people. I hope to meet them before the two weeks is up."

Arnav opened the screen door and stepped inside. "Okay, you're not going to believe this."

Jai followed him, carrying a plate piled high with sizzling steak and chicken.

"What?" Foster opened the fridge, grabbed a bunch of bottles of salad dressing, and put them on the counter. "Serve yourselves."

"I totally forgot that Minal said Parvan is at Pride Camp." Arnav grinned. "Jai didn't mention him by name, but I suddenly realized..." He met my gaze. "Minal is the youngest of my many sisters. Her husband's nephew is at Jai's camp. Isn't that cool?"

I met Jai's gaze. I wasn't reading ease—nor was he as uncomfortable as he'd been initially. I didn't see a conflict of interest—he clearly wasn't sharing anything personal about my kid—or the other kids. We weren't dating.

Hell, I wasn't even sure if he knew who I was. Much of the time, I thought not. But then he'd look at me a certain way, and I was sure he remembered.

"What kinds of dressing do you have?" I meandered over, eyeing the green salad with lettuce, tomato slices, green peppers, and shredded cheese.

"Ranch, Caesar, Italian, Thousand Island, and Blue Cheese."

Jai and I both winced.

"Blue cheese?" My gaze shot between Foster and Arnav.

Foster pointed to Arnav who shrugged. "In my defense, I don't *love* it. But eating it pisses Rashmi off, and that alone is worth the price of admission."

At my frown, Jai actually smiled. "Rashmi is the...least strident of the sisters."

"Oh really." Foster's eyes widened.

Jai cocked his head.

Arnav hooted, then threw his arm around him. "My friend, has the world changed since you've been gone."

"Oh." For a moment, Jai appeared...disconcerted.

"It's all good." Foster grinned. "I only know her as..." He winced. "I'm trying to think of an adjective that's not going to get me into trouble..."

"Friendly? Courteous? Kind." I didn't know Rashmi, but surely she could be one or more of those things.

"Right. All of the above." Foster's brow unknit—clearly from relief. "And honest. Rashmi is nothing if not honest."

Another hoot from Arnav. "Oh, that's so true." He grinned at Jai. "You're coming for dinner one Saturday night with the family." He pivoted to me. "You too."

I blinked.

"Jai will need someone to protect him from Rashmi while Mama fawns over him." Arnav rolled his eyes. "Jai always was her favorite."

"I'm not sure—" Jai started to speak.

"You have no idea how often Mama would say, *why can't you be like that good boy, Jai?*"

"Oh. I didn't know that."

He wagged his finger. "And don't go thinking this was because I was gay. I was just...a hellraiser. Came from having six older sisters."

"You were spoiled." Foster handed me a plate and gestured to the food.

Green salad, corn, mashed potatoes, barbecue chicken, as well as steak.

"I don't even know where to start." I eyed the food.

Jai smiled. "From the beginning. Let me tell you about the first time I met Arnav."

Foster perked up.

Arnav rolled his eyes.

I straightened. Sure, I was curious about Arnav's childhood. I was more curious about Jai, though. How he'd grown up. And I was quite certain he wouldn't be able to spill the beans about his friend without revealing more about himself. So I was all ears.

Chapter Seven

Jai

"I can't believe I left these in the car." I retrieved the bag of dog treats from my front seat. Fortunately the weather wasn't too hot, so I didn't have to worry about the treats overheating.

Arnav grinned as he held leashes for the two dogs. Demetrius had offered to clean the kitchen—one of my least favorite tasks.

Foster had tried to say something about guests, but I'd suggested Arnav and I could walk the dogs.

Demetrius said that sounded fair and perhaps Foster could sit on a stool at their kitchen island and tell him how to do things properly?

I figured the guy was pretty swift and could clean up a kitchen without direction—but this gave him a bit more alone time with Foster. Even I, who could sometimes be a little dense, noted how quickly the men appeared to have...bonded. I didn't figure just their shared skin color was the reason. No, Demetrius made Foster laugh. I hadn't thought it all that unusual until Arnav, during our walk, explained that Foster was normally reserved and shy.

"Well, less so since I burst into his life." Arnav was clearly pleased with himself.

"How did you meet?" Mission City was small enough for two gay guys to encounter each other. But although Arnav had always been out and proud—well, since he was twelve—Foster, by his own admission, hadn't come out until Arnav had kissed him on the cheek in Fifties.

Arnav had winced and said he hadn't meant to out Foster.

Foster assured him that he didn't mind. *You presented me with the chance to be myself. For the first time in my life.* He'd said the words with a grin on his face.

That resonated with me. *What would it be like if I could be my true self? With someone who accepted me?*

"Okay...so I asked Foster if he minded me telling you our secret." Arnav snagged the bag of dog treats. "Oh God, these are Queenie's favorites. And Taffy will eat anything Queenie eats. So I'll let you give them one. Just one. I don't want Taryn and Stephanie to come home to find their dog has gained a lot of weight."

"I think it's great you have a lesbian couple living next door."

"Well, you should meet Stephanie's brother, Cooper. Holy Lord. You think I'm loud and proud? Cooper has me outdone by a mile."

"Oh?" I snagged Taffy's leash.

"Right? And then there's Taryn's brother Lachlan. Pretty much the complete opposite of Cooper. He's an entertainment lawyer from Toronto. Great guy. Oh, I have to show you—" He handed me the bag of treats as well as Queenie's leash.

Both dogs gazed at me expectantly.

Then Arnav held his phone for me to see.

I squinted. "Okay, you're going to have to explain."

He grinned. "The women had an *Alice in Wonderland* themed wedding. So adorable. Stephanie was Alice, Taryn was the Mad Hatter, Lachlan was the White Rabbit, and Cooper—"

"Was the Queen of Hearts?" I squinted again.

"Yep. Now, that's brotherly love." He put his phone away. "I love my sisters, but I would never wear that getup for any of them."

"But you would if one of your nibblets asked." I used the non-gender specific term for nieces and nephews.

Arnav glared as he took Taffy's leash. "You just had to go there." He wagged his finger. "Do *not* tell Parvan. He'll tell Minal, she'll tell the other five, and somehow I can see myself wearing a sari."

I grinned at the image. "You'd look good in a sari."

He pursed his lips. "I'm going to save the witty comeback for another time. I'll need it more if you coerce Foster and gang up on me."

"Hey."

"Hey, what? I seem to have been the butt of several jokes over dinner."

His words had me hesitating for a moment until he broke into a broad grin.

"I would've said something if I actually minded. You seemed super stressed when you first arrived. And yeah, I should've mentioned I'd invited Demetrius. That was my bad."

I wouldn't have come, and I would've missed out on this wonderful evening.

"All good."

Queenie eyed us. Well, and the bag of treats.

"They can have one each when we take them inside." Arnav held up the poop bag. "I'll deal with this in the garage; you go ahead through the front."

"Sure. That sounds great." Because I really didn't want to deal with dog shit. *Admit it, if you had a dog, you would totally scoop the poop.*

Points for honesty.

Kennedy was bringing her therapy dog, Tiffany, to the camp tomorrow.

None of the campers had allergies nor expressed a fear of dogs.

The yellow lab had a placid nature—I'd met her twice—and I hoped offering everyone a chance to enjoy some canine companionship would be a good thing.

I entered the front door, closed it firmly, unclipped the leashes, then shooed the dogs. Encouraged them into the hallway toward the kitchen. Tried to get them moving.

Their gazes remained riveted to the bag.

I sighed. "Okay, let's go." I led the way to the kitchen accompanied by clacking nails on the hardwood.

Upon spotting Foster, who turned to watch us come in, I smiled. "You never have to worry about being caught unaware." During the tour of the lovely house, I'd discovered—aside from some throw rugs—there wasn't any carpeting in the place.

Foster, seated at the kitchen island, grinned. "You would be absolutely correct. I swear Queenie is extra loud. Especially around mealtime. Oh, are those dog treats?" He gestured to the bag in my hand. "Those are Taffy's favorite and Queenie's second-favorite."

"How can you tell?"

Foster spelled out a word. Clearly the name of a dog treat, but I didn't know that one and so was lost.

Queenie, however, was also lost. As in lost her ever-loving mind.

"Quick, give her one of those." He grinned.

I ripped open the bag.

Both dogs stilled.

I pulled out two treats. "Okay, sit."

Taffy plopped onto her butt.

Queenie did not.

"Uh..."

"Queenie, sit." Foster's voice carried a surprising amount of strength.

Nothing.

"Queenie, sit." Arnav spoke as he came into the kitchen.

The dog eased to a sitting position.

Foster groaned. "How is it that you're the softie when it comes to, uh, generous gifts, and they only listen to you?"

I gave the dogs their treats.

Arnav laughed. "Sweetheart, I think you answered your own question. They listen to me precisely because I'm, uh, generous—"

"You spoil them." Foster arched an eyebrow.

"I know how to put misbehaving puppies in their places."

Foster and Demetrius burst out laughing.

I stilled. *They don't know anything. They can't know anything. Because you haven't... Shit.* Yes, shit. Arnav and Foster had spoken to my mother. Undoubtedly, she'd told them everything— *Wait. Just calm the fuck down. Arnav would've said something. During the walk...he would've broached the subject.* We'd talked about several other personal things, so perhaps that logic applied.

"Dog treats are the best." Demetrius met my gaze. "That was very generous of you."

I swallowed my rising panic. "Arnav said not to bring anything...but he sent me a picture of the dogs. I wasn't certain which to pick..."

"You made a good choice." Demetrius smiled. "I find pups do what they're told when they're offered rewards. Treats."

Heat crept up my neck.

"Arnav." Foster gave his husband a little wave.

"Yes, my sweet."

"Turns out Demetrius shares your love of pups."

Arnav's eyes lit. "Oh wow. You ferreted that out?" He cocked his head to Demetrius. "He doesn't share that with everyone."

Demetrius continued to hold my gaze. "So this house is a safe space. I admit to being surprised—"

I dropped the bag of treats. "I have to go."

Incredibly grateful I hadn't been asked to remove my shoes—I bolted for the door. I shoved it open and practically ran to my SUV. I was inside in a heartbeat and tearing out of there as fast as I could.

He knows. I don't know how he knows...but he knows. Now Foster and Arnav know. And their house might be a safe space, but I can't ever go back there.

When the light finally turned green, I hung a left onto Cedar Street and began the climb. Up into the hills of North Mission City that would lead me away from town and to the sanctuary of the camp.

You need to remember to breathe.

No one actually said that Foster was a pup and that Arnav and Demetrius were...

I struggled for the right word.

Probably because I'd never had...one of my own. I didn't like *Master*, but would've accepted it. If I'd met the right person. I preferred Daddy. Which had all kinds of baggage attached to it. But I saw Daddies as benevolent and kind. Nurturers.

The opposite of my parents.

I'd met generous Daddies. Playful Daddies. Warm and loving Daddies.

As I continued the drive into the night, I blinked back tears. *Stupid. Stupid. Stupid.*

That nice Daddy told you not to call yourself stupid.

A memory long-suppressed.

All my time from the What'sUp Pup group had been shoved down. Put into a place in my mind—and my heart—where I never went. I refused to remember those idyllic nights when I went to Pup Night at the club and just enjoyed myself. When I could be free of all the stressors in my life.

High-powered job.

Demanding parents.

Cruel boyfriend.

Okay...to be fair. Gary hadn't been cruel during the relationship. Only when he'd discovered my secret—and told the entire world, including my parents—had his true colors shown.

I'd never cheated on him. Never looked at another man.

Had I fantasized about a relationship with a Daddy rather than a coworker who preferred we refer to each other as roommates?

Yep.

If I could've found a full-time Daddy, I probably would've left Gary.

Which didn't say much for our relationship. Which he'd absolutely torched when he shared my secret with everyone.

Thank God I'd gone in costume every night. Apparently WhatsUp Pup had closed and Pup Night had been folded into Club Kink. And guess who owned Kink? The benevolent benefactors of Pride Camp. Smith and Alessandra shared that news with me, just in case it became an issue with any of the parents.

To me, there was logic. LGBTQ folks came from far and wide—and flocked to Kink as their safe space.

The couple had seen that. Spotted the wounded souls who, had they received affirmation early on, might not have faced such trauma.

So Pride Camp was their attempt to provide a safe space for teenagers to figure out how they were going to face the world as a queer person.

If only...

Alas, regrets wouldn't get me far.

I pulled into the lot at Pride Camp and sild into my allotted spot.

Lights from both the great hall and several dorm rooms were visible in the moonlit night.

Should I go over to say hello? No, I don't want to intrude. I'd checked my phone repeatedly, but nothing from Grey, Makenna, or Cody.

Naturally, that prompted me to check again.

—I'm here if you want to talk about what happened tonight. Whatever it was, if I triggered it, I'm sorry. —

Arnav.

And a second text.

—Foster is sorry too. He doesn't normally share certain parts of himself. I was surprised. —

Finally.

—Sleep well. —

Right, like that was going to happen.

Chapter Eight

Demetrius

"I'm sorry you're having a rough go." I pressed my hand to Keegan's shoulder.

When he was younger, this soothed him.

I waited for him to shrug me off. To claim he didn't need to be babied anymore. He never did, though. He continued to need support from me. And, of course, he'd always have it.

Cody nodded his approval. "Maybe you want to tell your dad what happened?"

Keegan drew in a deep breath and finally met my gaze. "I'm sorry."

"For what?" I was baffled.

"You shouldn't have had to come." He glanced at Cody. Well, more like glared.

Cody held his gaze. "Your dad specifically asked that we call him if you had a panic attack. He respects your desire to handle them on your own, but he also needs the assurance that seeing you in person will bring to him. He loves you so much, Keegan."

"Yeah." I again squeezed his shoulder.

This time, he did shrug me off.

I didn't feel hurt.

Or so I told myself.

"You were the one who said I had to learn how to deal with them." He met my gaze.

"Not on your own." I tried to smile. "Keegan, you're thirteen. I know you want to be all grown-up—but you're not. And you've been through so much—"

"Don't bring Mom into this."

Ouch. Sometimes he still blamed her for getting sick and leaving him *alone*. I never pointed out he had Alaina and me.

"I wasn't going to." I gazed into those crystalline-blue eyes. So like his mom's. "I meant the stuff you've gone through at school. No kid should have to endure what you have. I think...while you're talking to Cody...that you should maybe consider going to a new school."

"That's just running away from my problems." Something else he was obsessed with—not being perceived as weak.

"No, it's not. Hell, it's not even a strategic retreat. It's called *a fresh start*. You're allowed to have one of those. To start anew and try again."

"The kids will all be the same."

"Hopefully that's not true." Cody straightened in his chair. "There are so many kids who are accepting. Who understand. Not so much in your dad's day—"

I snickered.

We shared a smile.

I pivoted my attention back to Cody. "You can try a different high school in East Van or we can look elsewhere. Maybe somewhere entirely new?"

"What about Alaina?"

"She's made it clear she wants what's best for you. Way more mature than any eleven-year-old should be. She's got a couple of close friends, but you remember Glynnis moved away in June. Alaina figures if she has to do the same, that's okay."

"Glynnis moved to Abbotsford." Keegan picked at his jean shorts.

"That's right. I forgot." *Where is he going with this?*

"Abbotsford is near Mission City."

"Yes, right across the bridge. I'll bet Glynnis's house isn't more than twenty minutes away." I held that thought in my mind for a very long moment. "So if we moved to Abbotsford or Mission City, then Glynnis and Alaina would be close again."

Keegan gazed at me and blinked several times.

I wanted to point out he'd only been here three days. That he'd been ensconced in a camp set up for kids like himself.

Except I'd met Aaron, Arnav, and Foster. All of whom had suggested Mission City was becoming a more-welcoming place. Aaron and Foster were both Black, like myself. Arnav was Indian. All implied they were mostly accepted for who they were. "This is a big decision. One we'd need to make as a family. I promise I'll talk to Alaina—if you still feel this way when she emerges from the wilderness."

"Promise?"

"I promise." I wasn't going to promise we'd move to Mission City—because that was a monumental decision—but I could promise to consider his request. I could honor the fact he was growing into a bright and brave young man. One who would always feel like an orphan—his word. I could love him forever, and he'd still feel loss.

I accepted that.

"Okay. Those are, I think, really productive discussions to have as a family." Cody smiled. "Now, why don't we talk about what happened?"

So we did. Turned out, Keegan had not been paying attention during a hike and had been startled by a racoon and screamed, then jumped and fell over.

He was horrifically embarrassed that a little gray, furry creature had set him off. But his mom always warned him about the critters—especially that they were vicious. And, living in East Van, having a respectful fear of the little shits wasn't a bad thing. Since racoons were mostly nocturnal, Keegan had never seen one in person.

None of the other kids had laughed at him. In fact, Paisley had tried to reassure him. But he'd been humiliated, and that had led to the panic attack which had spiraled out of control.

Cody had intervened and guided Keegan away from the group.

Keegan asked for me in the middle of his attack.

I'd dropped everything to get here as quickly as possible, repeating over and over in my mind how glad I was to have chosen to stay in Mission City.

Except Keegan wasn't pleased I'd come running, even though he'd asked for me. Once he was out of the crisis, he was embarrassed.

Now, he said he might want to move here.

I didn't know how to react to that.

So I held my thoughts to myself.

Cody gently asked Keegan about what had happened during the school year. And, to me, why I'd reached out to employee assistance.

Never had I been more glad for my employers and their generosity in providing free, anonymous counseling for their employees.

After about twenty minutes, Keegan checked his watch. "It's about lunchtime."

"You're hungry?" Sometimes, when he was upset, he didn't want to eat.

"They're serving pierogies."

"Ah." *Well, he loves them and you can just take this as a good sign.* "That's awesome. I might have some one night this week when I go to Fifties." I met Cody's gaze.

He grinned. "Best burgers in Mission City, but their pierogies are amazing as well."

"And blueberry milkshakes." I grinned right back.

"Ew." Keegan scrunched his nose.

Cody and I laughed.

Then the psychologist waved toward the dining hall. "You go ahead, Keegan. Is it okay if I talk to your dad for a few minutes?"

Keegan looked uncertainly between the two of us, but finally nodded. "Yeah, that would be okay. I'm going to go find Paisley."

Another good sign.

Cody saw him out, then closed the door and returned to his seat.

I cocked my head.

"Nothing so serious. I just wanted to say I think you're doing a fantastic job. I mean, I don't know the ins and outs of your daily routine, but Keegan speaks highly of you. In one breath, he emphasizes he's an orphan. In the next, he talks about his *amazing* dad." He put the words in air quotes.

"I try, Cody. So damn hard. I love the kids and only want what's best for them. I'm hoping this place is what's best for him."

"He's safe here. Racoons aside, of course."

I chuckled. "At least it wasn't a skunk.

"Also nocturnal creatures. Frankly, I was surprised we saw a racoon at all. Although, my aunt lives about three miles from here and she's got a family on her property. They're abundant around here."

"I assume they forage for actual food instead of trash?"

"Oh, both. Hence needing secure containers for compost and garbage. Although, frankly, the bears are much tougher. They're smart too. Can get into anything."

I swallowed. "And they're around here?"

"We haven't spotted any. That said, there've been sightings around the area recently. Big, black bears. We spent some time with the kids, letting them know what to do. We have rules about going out by oneself or even just in pairs."

All of which I knew—but hearing it repeated helped ease my mind. "Thanks, Cody."

"I can't even imagine being a single dad—let alone a widower *and* a single dad."

"Uh..." I frowned. "I miss Erlene a lot, but I'm truly focused on the kids. They're my everything."

"Which is so very clear. They're lucky to have you."

His comment felt overwhelming—he didn't know what our lives were at home. I did my best to be a good dad, but I wasn't perfect. Still, if he said he knew I was putting in every effort to make life easier for the kid? That had to mean something.

"I'll get going." I rose.

Cody did as well. "We're taking care of him. I appreciate you came so quickly."

"Never will hesitate. Hell, racoons are nasty creatures." I shuddered. I'd encountered several in a back alley once. They'd pried open a garbage can and had made a gratuitous mess. Just...vile.

And yet I understood they had a place in the food chain.

And were occasionally roadkill.

Gross.

When we exited the counselor's office, he pointed toward the great hall. "I need to get going."

"I can see myself out."

"Great." He waved and hustled away.

I eyed the administration office. *Just to see if he's there.* To say how lovely last night had been. To ask him if we might do coffee.

Or something.

Was that still a thing? I'd lost the thread so many years ago. I used to date. Somewhere between Imani finishing grad school and Erlene getting sick.

Men, women, in-between. I wasn't picky. If they were friendly, I was more than happy to spend time with them.

Especially puppies and other Daddies.

I approached the administration office.

Spotting no one, I knocked on the door.

When no one answered...I nudged the handle.

Unlocked.

Okay, so that was a sign.

Right?

I pushed my way into the office and let the door close behind me with a snick.

No one was in the outer office space, so I moved to Jai's office and knocked. And waited. And knocked again.

The door wasn't even closed properly.

Which worried me, because I spotted a laptop on the desk. Oh, it was attached to a cable. Not impossible to steal, but definitely harder.

I removed the present from my pocket and placed it on the desk.

With a grin, I slipped out.

I closed the office door, strode to the outer door, let myself out, and then headed to my car.

Darn pleased with myself.

Chapter Nine

Jai

This is rewarding. This is rewarding. This is...

Exhausting.

Being a counselor for the last five years at other camps had given me a sense of how fatiguing camp could be. Kids who wouldn't go to sleep. Kids who wouldn't wake up. Time in the fresh outdoors. Forced to be inside when the weather turned.

I'd seen it all.

Being responsible for ten souls plus staff?

Overwhelming.

Every moment felt like a struggle because, rightly or wrongly, I felt everything rested on my shoulders.

My bed beckoned—

Damn. I didn't put away my paperwork.

I headed over to the administration building and was horrified, upon trying the door, to find it unlocked.

How...?

You were thinking about Demetrius. About how much fun you had last night. Once you got over your nerves, anyway. And how you ran away like a headless chicken.

And apparently had forgotten to lock the administration building.

I wasn't really worried about the campers. They didn't seem like the type for hijinks. The staff would obviously keep away. So unless someone had come onto the property...

My office door was at least closed—although not locked.

Overall, I hoped nothing bad had happened.

I opened the door and headed to my desk.

And stopped short.

My breath caught.

My gaze darted around the room—as if the answers were contained within these walls.

Panic rose within me.

You have to breathe. No one will come to your rescue if you have a panic attack.

Keegan's episode earlier in the day had been a sober reminder of my past. Of that period immediately after I'd left Vancouver. When my life had fallen apart. Although actual panic attacks had been rare, I'd lived with a gnawing sense of fear for all these years.

Slowly, I advanced to the desk.

Dog treats and a little chew toy.

To be precise, my favorite dog treats and a chew toy identical to the one I'd had all those years ago.

Six years is not that long ago. You tell yourself that you're old...but that's not exactly true.

Because, in this moment, all those panicky feelings returned with a vengeance. Clearly someone knew who I was. Had remembered me from all those years ago. Except that made no sense, so the alternative was someone had spoken to Gary. Except that didn't make sense either because, although he knew I liked to dress up like a dog and play with other puppies, he didn't know my favorite toys and treats. Treats made for dogs, but that could be eaten by humans. Toys that squeaked.

I grabbed my messenger bag and shoved them in. I removed the laptop from the docking station—to which it had been locked securely—and I put that in my bag as well. I would have to disconnect it from the Wi-Fi and run it through a virus protection program because I had no way of knowing if someone had come in here and attempted to access the data. My heart caught in my throat.

Nothing appeared out of place. I didn't keep paper files on the kids—or even notes. Cody had password-protected files that only he, Alessandra, and Kennedy could access. I had an admin override, but that was only for dire emergencies. And only if I couldn't reach any of the three who had access.

I should've been relieved—but I wasn't. I'd screwed up badly. *Do I call Alessandra and let her know? How bad of a mess is this? Did someone see who came into the office?*

We had cameras along the edge of the property line—in case someone tried to get in to cause damage. But we'd opted not to have them in the camp itself. People might feel like every moment of their lives was recorded, but here we tried to make it a safe space. Where campers could be themselves and not worry.

I ensured my office windows were fastened and secure before locking the door to my office. Once I had all the lights turned off, I exited the building and bolted that door as well.

No one was about.

After today's morning hike and afternoon swimming, I hoped—once campfire was over—the teens would be ready for lights-out.

Finn, the firefighter who lived nearby, had stopped in yesterday to let me know the municipality was eyeing a campfire ban next week.

We'd been particularly dry in the late spring, with almost no precipitation for the last month. Everyone hated the bans—but they hated wildfires way more. Tonight was to be our one and only campfire.

I unlocked my cabin door and slid inside, quickly relocking it. I hadn't been in here all day, and hadn't been running the air conditioning, so a warmth lingered. After putting my laptop bag on the dining room table, I set about opening all the windows. The screens would keep out the bugs, but hopefully some of the cooler night air could waft in. I eyed the ceiling fan and decided not to turn it on.

The gross, sticky sweat that had soaked me upon finding the *gifts* someone had left for me was now turning my skin cold and clammy. I secured the laptop in the wall safe, then headed into the bathroom.

Clear planning had gone into the design of this cabin. A four-piece bathroom was positively decadent, and I headed to the shower. The compact bedroom offered privacy, while the much-larger main room allowed for entertaining of up to six.

What had Alessandra been thinking? I had no idea when I'd ever be entertaining six people. Perhaps the next director would be more social.

I stripped and turned on the faucet. The hot-water-on-demand feature was appreciated, and soon I was under hot spray.

My mind whirled.

The image of the toy and treats were imprinted on my mind.

Who would know? Why would they threaten me with exposure? Why not just out me and get it over with? I'll be let go from the camp for certain—

That thought circled. Alessandra and Smith were kinky. Perhaps they would be more understanding of someone else whose...predilections...were more closely aligned with theirs.

Not all kinky people respect age- and puppy-play. Oh, and kitty-play. We'd had two cats who enjoyed coming to pup night. They tended to stick to their corner but could, with the correct inducement, be pulled into play. Usually a large ball or yarn or a laser pointer were required. *Those were good times. Really good times.*

Then Gary had discovered what I was doing in my spare time while he was off wining and dining clients on his expense account. That part of the job never appealed to me. I chose to stick to financial analysis and leave the selling to guys like Gary.

I'd never ascertained how he'd uncovered my secret. But one night I came home from the club to discover he'd gone through my private things. *Stupid to believe he'd ever respect artificial boundaries.* Except they hadn't felt artificial to me—he had his space, and I had mine. I kept a suitcase at the back of my closet with my pup stuff. I'd come home to find it strewn across our bed.

Almost a sacrilege.

I shampooed my hair, using my nails in my scalp.

Any hope of containing the damage had been in vain.

He'd already called my parents, all the coworkers he could, as well as the managing partners of the accounting firm we worked for. I'd been gone just three hours, and in that time, he'd managed to destroy my life.

I'd packed a bag and gone to a hotel.

The next morning, when I'd shown up for work, my laptop had been confiscated, along with my security pass, and I'd been shown the door. One senior partner, Hazel, hadn't looked pleased. The three male partners, along with Gary, had been smug—clearly basking in their superiority.

Yeah, but what secrets did they hold?

Why hadn't I found the courage to fight back?

Gary wasn't in the closet...but he also hadn't been out. How he'd explained finding my puppy paraphernalia while carrying on the illusion we were *just roommates* was beyond me. Or maybe he hadn't. Who knew?

I'd gone back to the apartment, packed all my things, and headed home.

Only to find my father barring my entrance and demanding I return the key. After being away for six years, I had few things remaining in their house—certainly nothing to fight over. So I got in my car and drove east.

Stop dwelling.

I rinsed my hair and then stuck my face under the spray. The warm water hit my skin, and I reveled in the heat.

Aside from rest breaks, I'd driven straight through to Toronto. More than halfway across the country.

Even that hadn't been far enough.

I quickly discovered I wouldn't be getting a reference from my old employer. No one was willing to risk a lawsuit at the old firm, but they made it clear my work hadn't been to their standards.

Which was total bullshit, but whatever.

Then I found the ad for a camp in Nova Scotia looking for counselors.

A Pride Camp.

Even without an interview secured, I drove there. I showed up with a résumé and, what the director later confided was a desperate appearance. She'd given me the job on the spot. At only twenty-three, I was barely older than most of the campers.

Six years ago.

I shut off the shower, shook off, then stepped onto the bathmat. I grabbed a towel and set about drying myself.

Going down memory lane isn't helping.

What if Gary did this? What if he heard about me coming back and...?

How would he have heard? What would he get out of this?

Too many questions and too few answers.

Once I was dry, I donned my pajamas and then dried my hair with the blow dryer. Then I brushed my teeth.

Just as I was about to turn off light, I looked into the mirror.

Why me?

I flipped off the light.

Whether I was asking why I enjoyed things that others found perverted or whether I was asking why I was being targeted, I wasn't certain.

I opened the safe and removed the laptop.

After putting it on the counter, I grabbed a soda from the fridge. I cracked the can and sat at the dining room table with the laptop. Although I didn't have mad computer skills, I'd studied enough programing in university to be able to start the machine in safe mode and to review the access logs.

Nothing looked amiss. No attempts since I'd last been on.

Just to be safe, I ran the machine through the virus detector. While it worked, I wandered into the kitchen. I wasn't hungry, but decided I really needed a snack as dinner had been a number of hours ago.

The sound of laughter carried through the open windows as the campers gathered around the firepit.

Might as well eat something sizable. No way will I be able to sleep with that noise.

Or with my mind going a million miles an hour.

I set about making a grilled cheese sandwich.

By the time that task was complete, my mind was a little more settled, and the laptop was ready to go. No malicious software found.

That brought a modicum of relief.

So I settled in to eat my snack and to review the schedule for the rest of camp—even though I'd already done it daily for two months since taking the job.

Anything to forget the treats and toy at the bottom of my messenger bag.

And how I might be on the precipice of losing this amazing life I'd built for myself.

Chapter Ten

Demetrius

I grinned at Aaron. "Arnav and Foster told you I have a weakness for White Spot." I sat in a booth across from the hotel manager and his husband, Noel.

"Far from it. We had our wedding reception here, so we're a little partial."

I arched an eyebrow. "Okay, that I didn't see coming."

Noel grinned. "I remember the first time I introduced him to Triple O's sauce."

Aaron groaned. "Died and gone to heaven."

This, I couldn't conceive. I loved it, but wouldn't have been quite so effusive with the praise. "Nothing like that in..." I squinted, trying to remember where Aaron was from.

"California."

"Right."

"Cataluma was known for strawberries, not amazing sauces."
Aaron shrugged. "And it definitely didn't have this guy." He nudged
Noel.

"So you came north."

"Love makes people do crazy things."

I wasn't going to argue with that. I'd seen a few people fall head over
heels in love in the past. Hell, I'd been pretty close to that with Erlene.
At least, that's what I told myself.

Lindsay arrived in time to take our very-clean plates. "Dessert menu
is there." She gestured with her chin.

"I cannot imagine having room for anything else." I rubbed my
belly.

Noel handed the menu to me. "Get something to go. You can eat it
later."

The Grand Hotel was small, and although I could go down to the
bar for grub, room service would've stopped serving by the time I
returned. Already, the sun was touching the horizon.

We'd been here for more than an hour.

"Well then..." I eyed the menu. "Oh, New York cheesecake."

"Blueberry, strawberry, or chocolate sauce?"

I licked my lips. "I had a blueberry milkshake yesterday at Fifties.
Oh, sorry."

She laughed. "They make great milkshakes. Their burgers aren't
bad either. Not as good as ours, mind..."

"No, for sure not." I crossed my fingers behind my back. Honestly,
I was grateful I wasn't a food critic who had to choose. "I'll take
chocolate sauce." I eyed the guys. "I should be able to eat it here." We
hadn't even started talking about the reason we were here tonight.

"Great. And you two?"

"Two slices of apple pie to go." Aaron eyed me. "We can't wait for blueberry season."

"My favorite time of year." I fingered my napkin as Lindsay took off. The first portion of the meal had been the *getting to know you better* part of the evening. I appreciated they hadn't just dived right into the adoption stuff. I'd said I was happy to share—which I was—but I preferred to know the people I was about to share my heart with.

"So I'd known Erlene for about ten years. We met through work—and just...clicked. Not in a romantic sense. She was dating a guy seriously back then. Just, we had a similar outlook on life. I was single and occasionally seeing people. She knew she wanted to be a mom more than anything. Truthfully, I was still supporting my sisters through school and just trying to keep my head above water."

"Your twin sisters, right?" Noel squinted. "Imani and Malaya."

"Yep. Amazingly smart. I'm not dumb, but I'm also not in their caliber of smarts. Easy decision for me to focus on working while paying for their schooling." My sisters had always been my top priority—pretty much from the day Mom had brought them home from the hospital and explained what being a big brother meant. More so after she, and then Nan, passed.

"I won't comment." Aaron offered a sympathetic smile. "I maintain my younger cousin Trey is way smarter than I am, and I was happy to take care of him."

He understood.

"About the time my sisters got their footing, Erlene was diagnosed with cancer. Her husband died five years earlier. So she had two kids and no extended family."

"She panicked, right?" Noel grasped Aaron's hand. "Dad, for all his faults, panicked when Mom died. Kendra and I were teenagers, but he still didn't know what to do."

"Panic's a good word. And, since I loved her, it made sense for us to marry."

The men exchanged a look I didn't understand.

"And then the cancer went into remission." Erlene wanted to let me go at that point, but I'd committed to her. She was the one who suggested I go to Pup Night. She understood that part of me. I'd never strayed, of course. Never formed any lasting attachments. I'd simply taken the opportunity to enjoy myself with other Daddies and pups.

"But the remission didn't take?" Aaron winced.

I shook my head. "It came back with a vengeance, and she was gone four months later. We didn't really have time to prepare the kids. Alaina was so damn young. Keegan older and therefore more aware of what was going on. I wanted to, I don't know, protect him? But he's such a bright kid, and he figured it out right quick. Erlene decided he could know what was going on. I've worried Alaina might resent the fact she wasn't in the loop, but it's never come up. We finally explained that her mom was dying. Then...the end."

Noel blinked.

This is probably bringing back memories of his mom dying.

Aaron squeezed his husband's hand.

Noel cleared his throat. "I had Kendra to take care of. My dad basically checked out, and I had a grieving younger sister. She, uh, went a little wild for a few years."

"But is settled now and about to become a mother." Aaron smiled. "Uncle Noel has a nice ring to it."

"And Uncle Aaron." He wrinkled his nose. "I just wish we could convince them to come north."

"Javier has a business in Cataluma—"

"He could open a pot shop up here." Noel pursed his lips.

I wasn't going to step into the middle of what was clearly an ongoing debate. "So then Erlene died."

"Ouch." Aaron gripped Noel's hand extra tight.

"I'd formally adopted the kids just a few months after we married—to make certain they were cared for. No one ever said anything when Erlene died, and the paperwork was all in order. Now, losing someone is fucking awful—" I cringed. "Sorry."

Noel waved me off.

"—and suddenly I had two grieving kids and my own pain to deal with. Oh, and I was a single father. I work from home, so I was able to juggle things a bit until things evened out. The kids went back to school, and I thought we were doing okay."

"Until?" Aaron leaned closer.

"Well, I mean, things are still *okay*. We're making do. I got the kids into counseling until their therapist thought they were coping as well as could be expected. Then, just a few months ago, things went sideways again."

"Oh?" Noel also leaned in.

"My boy was being bullied at school. It's sort of a long story, but we're in Mission City to get him some help. I only pray we can get things back on track. Or maybe find a different track...?"

Aaron cocked his head.

"He says he wants to relocate to Mission City. From East Van—the home he's known his entire life."

"Did it occur to you he might be wanting a fresh start?" Noel blinked his blue eyes.

"Or that he's trying to escape more than just bullies?" Aaron's contribution.

I frowned. "You mean like memories and stuff?"

"Could be." Aaron appeared to consider. "Life can be tough for kids. Sometimes a do-over, or something like that, is a good thing."

"Okay."

"Cheesecake." Lindsay placed the plate before me as well as boxes for the men.

"Thank you. This looks amazing." I was always grateful for whomever served me.

"My pleasure." She surveyed the table, clearly gauging our drink levels.

"I'll take a refill." Noel grinned. "Thanks."

"Cola, right?"

He nodded.

She took the empty glass and headed back toward the kitchen.

I poised my fork over the dessert.

"You go ahead." Aaron linked hands with Noel. "We weren't certain about becoming parents. I'm no spring chicken."

I figured the guy was a year or two older than me, but I held my tongue about what a load of bullshit that was.

"With Kendra being pregnant, though, we've had a rethink." He nudged Noel. "We'll be named guardians should anything happen to Javier and Kendra. Of course, we never want that to transpire. We're hoping they have happy and fruitful lives."

"But it got us thinking." Noel held my gaze. "What about kids who need a home? I know the government tries to keep families together, but things happen. And what about the kids who don't have anyone? We could offer them a place."

"We're not picky about age." Aaron met Noel's gaze before turning his attention back to me. "Like, how about teenagers whose parents kick them out for whatever reason—"

"Being gay." I forked another piece of cheesecake.

"—being gay." He smiled, but his eyes held sorrow. "Or if there are younger kids, we'd be happy to take them as well. We'd prefer to think long-term, but if kids just need a safe place for a short period of time, and we can offer that, why would we not?"

"We've got a couple of spare bedrooms." Noel shrugged. "We've considered making them more kid-friendly."

"You two sound like you've got your act together." I mixed some chocolate sauce with the crust. "There's no manual. I mean you can read a million blog posts and books and all that crap. But when you've got a kid who's hurting, your instinct is to fix it. Sometimes you can do that, and sometimes it's not possible. I love that you're open to taking in any kid who needs help. That's a tough thing—especially when you know they're not going to stay. I thought—" I swallowed the lump in my throat. "—when Erlene recovered, I thought she might ask me to leave. She didn't, though. Even though we married because she was sick, we were committed to each other. To the kids. And that was that."

Aaron nodded. "You're a good man."

"I did what needed to be done. Zero regrets. I didn't grow up assuming I was going to be a father. What with Mom getting sick—and then Nan—I had enough to deal with. Getting my sisters settled in life was my priority. Once that happened, I was open to what might come next. Erlene came next and there's nothing I would've done differently. Now I just need to focus on the kids and what they want. What they need."

Noel cocked his head. "What about you?"

"What about me?" I frowned.

"It's just...I get about putting the kids first. But you're still a person. Don't you want to remarry?"

I blinked. "Let me get the kids through university, and then I'll think about it."

Even as I repeated the words I said to anyone who asked about my personal life, the image of Jai flashed in my mind. He might be someone who could change my mind. But I had no idea if he'd want more than a Daddy/pup relationship. Hell, I didn't even know if he was in a relationship right now. *Huh. Maybe you should have figured that out* before *leaving him the treats?*

Oops.

"Maybe Mission City could be a fresh start for you as well." Aaron eyed me. "I'm certain we could find a nice woman to set you up with."

"Or a man." I shoved the last of the cheesecake into my mouth.

"Bi?" Noel's curiosity was clearly piqued as he raised an eyebrow.

Mouth full, I merely nodded.

"Well, I'm pretty sure we could find a nice man to set you up with as well—our bad for assuming."

I shrugged, swallowed, and grinned. "I'm actually pan. Not a ton of dating experience, though. First helping my sisters, then Erlene, now, the kids…"

"Well, neither of us are matchmakers." Aaron grinned. "Oh, if you go to the library, be careful about sharing your single-and-available status with the librarian."

Noel chuckled. "Loriana has been trying to set people up forever. She's, uh, really bad at it."

"Long red hair, lovely dark-brown eyes, married to a computer technician named Mitch who is just the sweetest guy." Aaron smiled. "He's a good guy who I've been happy to get to know. He's like me—not from around these parts."

"Yes, but once you move here, it's really hard to move away." Noel offered me a sheepish shrug. "Small-town living. You either find it intrusive and annoying or you love it." He squeezed Aaron's hand. "We love it."

Their happiness carried me all the way back to the hotel. I wanted to call Jai to see if he got my gifts, but I wouldn't. I still had almost two weeks.

Plenty of time to figure out how I felt about him.

And how he might feel about me.

Chapter Eleven

Jai

"Are you excited about family day?" Grey offered his signature boyish grin.

"I am." Long debate had gone into whether we'd do this—for two reasons. First, if campers were here to get away from their parents, bringing those parents in might be painful. Secondly, not all parents could attend. We worried that might make campers feel excluded.

Gavin wasn't the least bit fazed that his parents were taking a long-planned trip to Italy—he'd been glad not to be dragged along.

Chris adored their parents, but was relieved they were visiting family in Yellowknife. Family who weren't always accepting of the *nonbinary* child.

Luli was a little sad about her mother not being able to make the day, but understood work had to be her mother's priority as she'd taken a lot of time off to deal with her daughter's issues.

As I surveyed the excited campers, Keegan stood out. He'd tried to play it off as cool, but he was clearly excited to see his father.

Parvan was grateful we limited guests to five. We were willing to make exceptions if the family had more siblings. Like, for instance, Arnav's family, where there were seven children. Parvan only had a brother and a sister. His extended family was massive, and all wanted to come and support.

I loved that, but limits made sense.

Grey nodded, then headed down to the group.

The debate had been whether or not Cody should make an appearance. Everyone knew he was the psychologist.

What had become apparent very quickly was how easily he fit into the group. Campers would look for him and wanted him to be included. *Is it because he's gay and they don't want anyone to be excluded, or does he provide a level of comfort and security?* I didn't know.

No one had asked about me when I wasn't around.

Which I was fine with.

Demetrius was the first to arrive—twelve minutes early.

Keegan was over to the minivan at a run, and the big man was barely out of the vehicle before he caught his son in his arms.

I hadn't perceived Keegan's distress as that high.

Cody caught my gaze and gave me a subtle nod. Ah, so this wasn't unexpected to him.

Parvan's family was next to arrive. Each member hugged him, and then they made it clear they wanted to meet everyone. Parvan might've rolled his eyes, but he was also clearly pleased at the interest his family showed in his new friends.

"How are things going?" Demetrius offered me a grin.

I'd spotted him greeting Parvan's family, but I hadn't noticed him peeling off from the group.

"I'm fine." I cleared my throat. "Keegan's doing well."

"I appreciate that...but your regular updates assure me of that. I'm asking how you're holding up—there's got to be a lot of pressure on you."

His intuitive understanding of my situation touched me in ways I didn't expect.

Alessandra and Smith checked in regularly—always assuring me I was doing a great job.

Cody kept an eye on me. He couldn't help himself.

I believed I was holding up fine. "We're planning for the next session."

Demetrius chuckled. "Keegan's annoyed you're limiting it to teens between fifteen and seventeen."

"Ah. I was under that impression. We're trying to keep the cohorts arranged by ages. I wasn't certain we could get twenty campers that age, but we did."

"And you'd better be operating next summer. Keegan's letter said he wanted to be a camper until he was allowed to be a counselor."

"That's great." *It means Demetrius will be here every summer. But will I?*

The toy and treats flashed in my mind.

"So..." Demetrius rubbed his chin.

His clean-shaven chin that appeared so smooth and that I totally wanted to caress with my fingers. "So," I prompted.

"I'd like to ask you out. You get nights off, right?"

This was an easy one. Disappointing, but an easy one. "I do have most nights off, but I'm not allowed to date parents of campers. Hard-and-fast rule."

He blinked. "That simple?"

I nodded. "I mean, I'm flattered..." *And hadn't even been certain you were gay, but now I know and doesn't that hurt.*

"Uh...no exceptions?"

"Nope."

"How about meeting a camper's father for a nice dinner—as a friend?"

"Appearance of impropriety. Of favoritism."

"I kind of want to call bullshit on that."

I might've bristled at the cuss word, but Isla and Francis's families had both arrived and the enthusiastic chatter even reached us where we stood, off to the side.

"Perhaps. But I don't make the rules."

"I'd like to see these rules."

I winced. "Uh, it's not written down."

"So there's nothing in writing that says you can't have a personal life?"

"That's a bit of an exaggeration. I enjoyed my time at the gathering the other night."

"Ah. So if I invite Arnav and Foster and we got together as a four-some..."

An image of Foster, Arnav, and Demetrius naked and in bed flashed before my eyes. "No." I sort of shot that out. Then I started coughing because I was choking on my spit.

"Are you okay?" Demetrius gazed at me with his unfathomable dark-brown eyes.

"Fine." I wheezed that.

"I'm not certain I believe you. But I'm not going to slap you on the back or give you the Heimlich maneuver or anything. I'm also not leaving you alone." He crossed his arms and continued to stare unblinkingly at me.

He had me completely unnerved and panicking. "I need to go." More coughing.

"I'm coming with you."

God, I can't catch a break. But I need a glass of water. Head held high—while still wheezing—I headed for my cabin. Once there, I pushed the door open and headed straight for the sink. I grabbed a glass, filled it with water, and started drinking.

"Hey, you might want to go easy—"

Demetrius's words cut off as I spit the water out into the sink. *Please, save me now.* Aside from when Gary had told everyone about my puppy persona, I couldn't remember feeling so embarrassed.

Even as I gasped, Demetrius put his hand on my back, between my shoulder blades. He hadn't asked me if he could touch—we had rules about consent—but I wasn't going to complain because that strong warmth at my back had me slowing my breathing. Had me trying to regulate my heart rate. Had me gradually trying to re-center myself.

I stared out the kitchen window to the forest beyond.

Don't miss the forest for the trees. Or is it don't miss the trees for the forest? What am I missing?

I always felt like there was something just beyond my grasp, and if I could reach it, then everything would be okay.

More fool you. You have a handsome man with his hand on you, and you're not taking advantage. I cleared my throat.

He didn't move his hand.

I nearly shrugged him off...except I liked the comfort he offered. "Thank you."

"You're welcome."

His deep, rumbly voice hit something deep inside me. "I'm not always incompetent."

"Never thought you were. You seem like a guy who's got his shit together."

"But—"

"No buts. You've got a lot of responsibility. And I'm offering you a night away from that. It doesn't have to be a date. I'm sorry you felt that was the only suggestion I was making. I don't do this often, so maybe I'm not as suave as I think I am."

That made me smile. I pressed back against his hand.

He held it secure.

"A night out as friends wouldn't be so bad."

"Great." He sounded genuinely enthusiastic. "We have the choice of Fifties, White Spot, Boston Pizza, Stavros's Greek, I think there's an Italian place. Oh, and the Chinese restaurant, the Indian place..." He paused. "And the Brew Pub. Or we can go over to Abbotsford—"

"Let's stick close." Even though that meant a greater chance of running into people I knew. Still, we weren't going on a date. *Or so you tell yourself.*

"Okay...which would you prefer?"

"You know, I grew up in Mission City, and I've never been to Stavros's."

"Okay. Now normally I would offer to pick you up, but since this isn't a date, why don't I just meet you there? It's within walking distance of my hotel. Say six o'clock? I can make a reservation."

Finally, I pulled away so I could meet his gaze. He was disturbingly close and had a woodsy scent. Interesting, because—as far as I knew—he hadn't spent any time in the woods today. "I can meet you at six. You can text or call if you change your mind."

He cocked his head. "Why would I change my mind?"

"Because, well, you're you..." I gestured up and down.

"What are you talking about?"

"You might get a better offer. There are other single folks in Mission City." I eyed him. "Oh God, I assumed you were asking me out on a date—"

"I was."

"—but I thought you were straight."

"Bi. Pan." He offered a broad grin. "People know I'm a widower and that she was the kids' mom, and they make the leap I'm straight."

"And I, of all people, should know about making assumptions."

He cocked his head.

I waved my hand to encompass the space. "Pride Camp."

"Well, I was taking a bit of a leap inviting you. Because you might be straight as well. I do my best not to assume. I thought, if you weren't inclined my way, that we could still have a night out."

I held his gaze. "One hundred percent gay."

Slowly, he nodded. "Do the campers know?"

"Parvan asked me. Super casual. Well, he made a comment about me being like his Uncle Arnav. I didn't contradict him."

"He might've meant you were both Indian."

"He might have...but he didn't. He was making the connection. I love that Arnav is part of his life—he's an uncle by marriage. When his sister realized her nephew was gay, she made that connection. All the family members involved are really supportive."

"Helps to have a gay uncle."

"A really cool gay uncle. Arnav has always been so sure of who he was and what he wanted."

"You think Foster was always part of that plan?"

I considered. "I know Arnav wanted to be seen as a competent lawyer, not a gay lawyer. But he's done some advocacy work as well as defense counsel and suing a couple of people. I hope people in town don't see him as the *gay* lawyer. Of course, he isn't the only one."

Demetrius arched an eyebrow.

"Alessandra hired Gil Herrington to do the foundation paperwork. He and his law partner Everett Williams are both gay. And Black."

"Oh."

"And married."

"Ah. Good to know. I'm finding more gay men—and more gay Black men—than I thought I would. Since Keegan started talking about moving here—"

"What?" My heart stuttered.

"Oh, right. Maybe you didn't know. Keegan really likes it here. I mean, he hasn't even been in Mission City proper, but everyone here he's met have him wanting to come here."

"There's still prejudice."

"I know that. I've been doing some investigation. Asking around. What I'm finding is that many people are accepting while some aren't. Some of those people are bible thumpers and some are just prejudiced. I also worry about Keegan having a Black stepfather."

"Those are valid concerns."

"Yes. So maybe over dinner you can tell me more about the good and the bad. I haven't made a decision yet. I also need to talk to Alaina to see where she's at. Her best friend just moved to Abbotsford, so she might be amenable to moving to Cedar Valley. It's a huge change."

A knock sounded at the door.

We stepped away from each other.

"Coming." I strode over to the door and opened it.

Cody stood on the other side. "Everyone's here and ready for lunch. I think you were planning to say a few words...?"

"Yes, of course. Mr. Fulton and I were..." I faltered. I didn't even know how long we'd been in here.

"Quickly discussing the potential move to Mission City." Demetrius came up beside me, but kept a decorous distance. "Mr. Prasad is from the town, and I thought I'd get his perspective."

Cody eyed us.

"As a person of color." I added that, then mentally slapped myself. Except maybe Cody would understand. He was Mission City born and bred...but he hadn't faced the discrimination Arnav and I had. The town might have plenty of South Asian people, but Caucasian was still the primary race. I was careful never to forget that.

"Understandable." Cody grinned. "I'm partial to the town. I went only as far as I needed to so I could earn my degree and come back. Plenty of kids in town to help. And not just gay ones." He met my gaze. "When you're ready."

"We'll come now." I gestured for the other two men to head out.

Once we were all outside, I locked the door.

As a group, we headed to the great room.

Chapter Twelve

Demetrius

I prided myself on always being early and arrived at Stavros's at ten minutes to six.

To find Jai outside, fidgeting.

Inwardly, I sighed. I'd hoped he'd be relaxed. Outwardly, though, I offered a wide smile. "Perfect timing."

He returned my smile. "I parked in the lot out back but then wasn't certain which way you'd be coming, but since you said you were coming from your hotel..." He gestured. "But then I realized I didn't know which hotel, because there are three—"

"The Grand."

"Which is what I figured because the other two aren't that close, and..." He winced. "I'm rambling."

I grinned. "I find it charming." I gestured to the door. "Shall we go in?"

"We're early."

"There's a seating area where we can wait." Truthfully, Stavros had been a little amused at me making a reservation for a Monday night. Apparently that was their slow night. "But I suspect our table will be waiting for us."

Stavros promised the perfect table and the best server.

I was touched.

The man himself greeted us when we arrived. "My friend Demetrius, so wonderful to see you."

My cheeks heated at his enthusiasm. "This is my friend, Jai."

"You are welcome here. Let me take you to your table. Best in the house." He grinned.

As Jai and I followed, I resisted the urge to put my hand possessively at his lower back. Yes, he'd responded to my touch earlier—but that had been in private. Tonight was public.

Well, for the five other occupied tables. Stavros hadn't been lying when he said Mondays weren't as busy. Still, Foster had mentioned Thursdays could be full and how he and Arnav had their first *unofficial* date here.

I'd smiled.

The best table was a booth set near the back—away from everyone else.

Jai slid in, facing away from the rest of the place, while I took the seat that afforded me a view. I couldn't imagine we'd run into anyone I knew, and this provided my companion with some semblance of privacy.

Stavros placed the menus on the table. "Water to start? Would you like a bottle of wine?"

"I don't drink." Jai met my gaze. "Sorry."

"Why would you be? I rarely have any. If it's okay, though, I might have one glass of red."

"Yes, please." He looked almost eager.

I turned to Stavros. "A glass of your house red would be perfect."

"I'll have an ice water." Jai offered a small smile.

"Wonderful. Timothea will be over shortly to take care of you. Only the best!" With a flourish, Stavros headed off.

Jai's eyes were wide. "Uh..."

"I asked for a reservation. We got to talking, and I said I was from out of town and..." I waved my hand. "Suddenly I feel like I made a new friend."

"One glass of house red." A slender woman with clear-blue eyes and long, black hair pulled into a ponytail placed the wine before me. "As Uncle Stavros said, I'll be your server tonight, and I'm to take extra-good care of you." She grinned impishly.

Right away, I liked her.

"And ice water." She flashed Jai a brilliant smile.

He smiled back.

Yep, she'd be getting a big tip. Anyone who made Jai smile deserved to be rewarded. He just didn't do it enough.

"I'll give you a couple of minutes with the menu."

"Actually..." I met Jai's gaze. "I thought we could get the Greek Platter for two, to share. Do you have any allergies?"

He shook his head.

"Anything you don't like?"

"Well, my mother was of the *eat what I put before you because of the starving children in Africa* school of child rearing."

I winced.

"Yeah. I have yet to find something I don't like. Oh, except pineapple on pizza. That's just gross."

I pressed a hand to my heart and gasped.

His face fell. His smile disappeared.

Before I could speak, Timothea was nodding frantically. "Right? I mean anchovies are better than pineapple—"

Jai and I both winced.

Our server laughed as she collected the unread menus. "If there's anything you don't wind up liking, we can swap it out. We just want you to be happy. I'll be back with pita bread and tzatziki in a minute." Then she was gone.

"Anchovies?" Jai scrunched his face.

"Yeah. Gross." I reached across to snag his hand, only pulling back at the last minute. "I was teasing about pineapple on pizza. Keegan feels the way you do. It's a friendly war between my kids and in the end, we usually wind up ordering two pies. Mine with, his without, and Alaina eating all the slices she can."

"That sounds...lovely." No missing the wistfulness in his voice.

"They also fight like cats and dogs. What with one being thirteen and one being a very mature eleven. I remember grade eight being the worst time of my school life, and Keegan's counselor confirmed eighth graders are the worst human beings on the planet."

"I can think of worse..." His eyes radiated sorrow.

"Oh, I'm sorry. I..." I had no words because I didn't know what had triggered him.

He waved me off. "Long story. Not why we're here tonight."

"Well, that's not true. I'm here to listen to whatever story you wish to tell. I want to get to know you. If I move to Mission City, you'll be my first official friend."

He cleared his throat. "I think Arnav and Foster—"

I shook my head. "You were the very first person I met. So if we become official friends, then you're number one. You'll always be number one." *God, please don't let that freak him out*. He was still so skittish—as his reaction to me this morning proved. *Maybe that was because you asked him out...?* And I still hadn't told him that I knew him from before. I hadn't ventured into that territory, since he clearly didn't recognize me.

"That's a really nice thing to say." Color slowly crept into his cheeks. "I still think Arnav and Foster should take that spot—you got invited to their house after one lunch."

I shrugged. "And I had dinner with Aaron and Noel last night. You might know Noel Barker. He's about your age. Or maybe a couple of years older. Great guy. Wound up following his sister to a small town in the States and falling in love with the innkeeper. Then he came back to Mission City, and the innkeeper basically followed him because he loves him too."

He blinked. "Just like that?"

"Yep. And now they're thinking about fostering, and they wanted to talk to me about what it's like to raise kids who are from your heart and not your blood."

"You're doing a great job."

I rubbed the back of my neck. "I don't always feel like it. I didn't realize how bad things had gotten for Keegan. I mean, he wants to move a hundred klicks just to get away from the bullies."

"He's met people who support him. He looks at Parvan, Paisley, Luli, and the others and thinks *that would be nice*."

"Is it?"

"Nice?"

I nodded.

He appeared to consider. "I think Arnav and I would see things differently when it comes to our experiences growing up in Mission City."

"How?"

"Well, he was out almost from the day he understood what that meant. Like, twelve or so. His family embraced and loved him. His mama lamented she wouldn't have grandkids from him, but by then several of his sisters were married or close to. God, he's got so many nibblets."

"And Parvan isn't even one of the *official* ones."

"True. But it's just like Arnav to take the kid under his wing. Being queer is tough. Being queer and Indian is doubly so." He eyed me.

"Same with being Black."

"Right. So I didn't come out. I just went along to get along, and only when I went to the University of British Columbia, and lived on campus, did I start experimenting. But nothing serious. Not until..." His eyes flashed pain.

"Greek platter for two." Timothea started laying out the plates of various dishes. The aroma wafted over me, and I grinned.

Jai didn't.

Fucking hell. Whoever not until *is, I want to kill the fucker.*

His pain hurt my heart.

Timothea, as if sensing the shift in mood, left quietly.

Jai blinked. "I'm sorry."

"Don't be. I'm the one who's pushing." I pointed to the calamari.

"Yeah, sure."

We each took a piece. Then we split the chicken souvlaki, dolmades, spanakopita, keftedakia, and rice. He indicated I should keep all the roast potatoes, and I magnanimously offered him the larger portion of the Greek salad. We dug in and several minutes passed as we devoured our food. Apparently, the veggie hot dogs and burgers of lunch were long forgotten.

Jai wiped his lips with his napkin. "I can't believe I've never been here. This is amazing."

"That's what Foster said when we discussed restaurants in the area. I'm trying to vary between fast food and nice dining while not breaking the bank."

"We're going Dutch tonight." He wrinkled his nose. "Can they split the platter for the bill?"

"I doubt it." I had no idea if this was true or not—but I wasn't going to let him pay for tonight. "You can pay next time. When was the last time you went to Fifties?"

"Never."

I blinked.

"We didn't eat out often." He held up his hand. "I lied. Arnav took me there. I had an amaretto milkshake."

"They make the best milkshakes. We need to go again. Do you have tomorrow night off?"

"You're here with me now, and you're already planning to see me again?"

"That's what friends do—they make plans. Normally I'd invite you over to my house to hang out, and I'd go to your place. You're obviously worried about the optics of being seen with a camper's father, and my place is currently a hotel room. Nice view, cute microwave, and an adorable mini-fridge. King-sized bed and friendly staff round out the amenities."

"I hope the friendly staff aren't *in* the king-sized bed." He pressed his fingers to his lips as color crept back into his cheeks. "That was very impertinent of me."

I hooted. "I think that's awesome. I'll have to tell Aaron, the manager. He'll laugh." I cocked my head. "I knew you had a bawdy sense of humor."

He paused with a forkful of calamari in the air. "How do you know that?"

Shit. "Because you just have this magnetic personality. I know you don't see it. *Not until* took that away from you, but I believe you can get it back."

"*Not until*...? Oh. Him." He shoved the fork into his mouth.

I bit into a dolma. *Don't push him. Let him come to you. You don't always have to be in a hurry to solve the world's problems.* Except I did. I saw injustice, and I stood up to defend. I witnessed wrongs, and I wanted to right them. Seeing people hurting also hurt me. I just had to be careful to only lash out at those causing the pain.

Jai swallowed. "His name was Gary. We met in our final year at UBC. We...hit it off. Then we applied for, and secured jobs at, the same accounting firm." He wrinkled his nose. "I didn't love working for high-net-worth clients, but I did enjoy the challenge and complexity of the files. Gary...? He was all about wining, dining, and securing bigger deals. He was flashy. I was...not."

"You mean you were reliable and hardworking. Not looking for credit."

He blinked. "Yeah, sort of."

"I know the type, Jai. Like your ex. I've met them. Taking credit for other's work. Coasting along doing the minimum while appearing to do more."

"Yeah."

"So what happened?"

Jai bit his lower lip. "He discovered something about me. Something incredibly personal. And he...shared that knowledge. With everyone. I mean *everyone*. I was ostracized, and I decided I needed a fresh start. I packed up my car and headed east."

His words hit me. Hard. Because unless he was talking about being gay—which he very well could be—he was also talking about being exposed as a pup.

Which explained *everything*.

"I'm so sorry that happened to you."

He toyed with his rice. "Long time ago."

"Six years?"

His gaze shot to me. "Yeah. How did you know?"

"Just a hunch." *Please let him believe the bullshit I'm shoveling.*

"Okay." He said the word slowly. Then he shook his head. "I got through it. And came out on the other end."

Without any family support and with few friends. As far as I could see.

Well, you've got me now, pup. I'm not letting you go.

Chapter Thirteen

Jai

*W*hy did I dump all that shit on him? Why the fuck did I tell him about Gary?

Questions I had no answers for.

As we lingered over baklava, those questions receded into the background. He drew me out by getting me to recall funny anecdotes from when I'd been a kid. Wait, there had been some? Oh, usually having to do with something Arnav had gotten up to. With six older sisters, one could be forgiven for thinking that with so many prying eyes, he'd be well behaved.

Nope. He loved to give his sisters a hard time. Especially Rashmi. The sister who was thirteen years older had been the bane of his existence, and they still went after each other on a regular basis. Or so he said when we'd gathered at his house. Whether he was exaggerating or not was an entirely different story because my friend could do that well.

Friend.

Demetrius laughed at a story I told—about a particularly interesting visit to the library where Arnav had been on the hunt for a book about gay sex, and the librarian, Loriana, had caught us. She hadn't been fazed, though. She'd found a book for my friend—which I might've also read later.

Timothea returned to remove our empty plates. "Coffee? Tea? Liqueur?"

We shook our heads.

"Just the bill." Demetrius offered her a genuine smile. After she left, he grinned at me. "Big tip."

"Well earned." We hadn't spoken about money. Pride Camp had a sliding scale so everyone who wanted to attend could—but he'd paid the full price for Keegan to come. That wasn't, relatively, a ton of money. Neither was it chump change.

Timothea arrived with the machine, and Demetrius paid. She wished us a goodnight and headed off.

"I feel like I need to walk off all that amazing food." Demetrius patted his flat stomach.

Does he have ripped abs under his shirt? Or does he have a little extra padding? Is his skin soft and smooth or rough? Chest hair or not?

As a teenager, I'd lamented at not having lots of body hair to make me manly. I'd wondered if that was part of the reason I was gay.

A couple of journal articles assured me I was *born this way*, and I moved on.

My chest hair did not, however, grow.

Gary used to say he liked the sparse look. Which, in the end, made me hate myself even more.

"Hey, are you okay?" Demetrius's brow furrowed in evident worry.

"Yeah, fine."

"You don't look fine. In fact, you look upset. Do you want to stay here and talk, or would you like to go for a walk? Downtown Mission City at dusk is lovely."

I glanced at my watch. We'd been here for almost three hours. *Huh.* "I should get going. You know…"

"Makenna, Grey, and Cody all have your phone number, right?"

"Well, yeah."

"And no texts or calls?"

I shook my head.

"So walk with me." He rose and held out his hand.

Without thinking, I took it. He guided me up and then let go and led me back toward the front of the restaurant.

"You gentlemen have a lovely evening." Stavros beamed.

"We had a lovely time. The food was perfection." Demetrius smiled right back.

"And Timothea was very attentive." I had to contribute.

"She's a good woman. I'm lucky to have her."

"I heard that, Uncle Stavros." Timothea pushed through the kitchen door with a tray of food. She grinned at us before heading to a table.

Stavros patted Demetrius on the back with a familiarity I found disconcerting. *Would he pat me on the back if I came back? Would I be okay with that? Or does Demetrius give off a vibe that makes it clear he doesn't mind?* Because plainly he didn't.

We headed into the evening—gray now, the sun having dipped out of sight.

"I love the fresh air. You just don't get this in the city."

I inhaled—something I'd never considered doing in downtown Mission City. Out at Pride Camp? All the time. In the city? No. "In the soupy summer days, the pollution hangs over the downtown."

"Oh, I didn't know that."

I nodded. "Not in the tourist brochures. My parents' house is just above the line, although it's all relative. Properties in the mountains have fewer issues. That's why Pride Camp's location is so awesome." *God, did I just say* awesome? *So lame.*

"Something to consider. I suppose I should look into finding a realtor."

"Oh, Arnav said…" I wracked my brains. "Cadence. Cadence Crawford." Even as I said the name, I laughed.

Demetrius cast a glance my way.

I pointed to the bench at the bus stop.

Cadence Crawford. Mission City's top realtor.

"Top realtor. Cool."

"I'd put more weight on Arnav's personal recommendation, myself. I mean, he and Foster spontaneously mentioned the guy. That's better than any award or…whatever."

We continued walking.

"So you're serious about moving?"

"Yeah, I think so. I mean, even just to put out some feelers. To see what I can get for the money I have saved. Plus, I'd sell the condo in East Van. I want to ensure there's enough for the kids' education, but I can borrow against the house. Or I might even be able to pay for their schooling myself. The one disadvantage of living this far from Vancouver is they might have to go away for college."

"There's a university over in Abbotsford. It's a great school."

"Oh, right." Demetrius appeared to lighten as the furrow in his brow disappeared.

"And some people take the commuter train into the city. It's a really long trip, but it's also an option—if they want to stay close to home."

"Plus, lots of virtual degrees these days. Both kids would have the discipline to do that."

"Then you have plenty of options." *Please move to Mission City. I need more friends.*

"Where are you going to live?"

"Huh?"

"When Pride Camp is over? Or will you live on the property year-round?"

"Honestly? I hadn't given it much thought. Alessandra's insisting on making mine a full-time position for the year. I'm free to pick up other work to supplement my income—when camp's closed—but she doesn't want to lose me."

"What would you do? Oh, what a lovely gift shop."

We halted and gazed through the display in the window. Lots of Indigenous art along with a few other unique items.

"I should get something for Alessandra. To thank her."

"That's a nice idea. Probably unnecessary, though."

"True." I bit my lip. "What do you buy a woman who is married to a billionaire?"

"Something one of a kind, I suppose. Or something for her cute kid. People always love that. Oh, is that a bookstore?"

We advanced to a stop a couple of doors down.

The Owl's Nest.

"How did I miss this earlier? Drat, they're closed."

"They've been here for as long as I can remember. I came in here a few times as a kid."

"I hope you enjoyed your visits." A deep voice came from behind us.

We turned to find two guys strolling up with creamy chills from Tim Horton's in their hands.

The slighter man—with blond hair and blue eyes—smiled. "I'm Dickens. My parents owned the shop before giving it to me. I've been running it for a while now." He focused his attention on me. "Jai, right?"

I nodded.

"You were a year behind me in school. You were friends with Arnav."

Again, I nodded.

"Well, I was a quiet kid. Always had my nose in a book."

"And I'm Spike." The taller man—with longish black hair and equally stunning blue eyes offered a shy smile. His T-shirt showed nice muscles. "If you have a motorcycle or vehicle that needs fixing, I'm happy to help."

Dickens nudged the man. "My husband is getting better at drumming up business."

"Well, I'm the best motorcycle mechanic in town." The man puffed his chest, even as his cheeks pinkened.

"Although MATH automotive gives him a run for his money in the vehicle repair department. Great women." Dickens continued to grin.

"Yeah, they are." Spike didn't appear the least bit upset at the suggestion he had competition from women.

"Would you like to come into the shop?" Dickens gestured.

"Oh, you closed a while ago." I'd noted the hours, thinking I might come back.

"Well, the great thing about being the proprietor is that I can do whatever I want. We went for our chilled treats and were planning to head home soon. But we can definitely spare a bit of time—no pressure to buy, okay? Browsing is allowed."

I cleared my throat. "I'd like to buy a book. For a toddler. I mean, the toddler can't read, but..."

Dickens nodded. "I know exactly what you mean. You can never start too early. Let's see what we can do." He unlocked the door, disarmed the alarm, and headed inside.

Spike held the door open and gestured for us to follow.

I went first, heading toward the counter where Dickens was turning on lights.

"So what might you be interested in browsing?" Spike eyed Demetrius. "I've gotten to know the place quite well."

"Do you have an LGBTQ section for teenagers? My son's a voracious reader, and I'd love to pick up a couple of books for him. Oh, and something about the history of Mission City. We might be moving here, and I'd love to know more about the place."

Spike offered a genuine smile. "I'm a transplant myself. Nothing like falling in love with a local and relocating. Although, I have to say I moved my business next door and *then* fell in love."

"Not love at first sight." Dickens wagged his finger. "Loud motorcycles."

"Yeah, but you love me."

"I do now." Dickens turned his attention back to me. "This way."

Nothing like falling in love with a local and relocating. I considered Spike's words. *Does he mean Demetrius and me? That he thinks that amazing man is in love with me? Huh. Do I explain or just let things ride?* Better not to say anything. One day the lovely couple would see Demetrius wandering down the main street with some other guy—or gal—and they'd realize they'd been mistaken.

Except the image of him with someone else settled like a knot in my stomach. I didn't want him with anyone else. To my shock, I wanted him with *me...*

"We have an amazing selection of picture books by local authors." Dickens beamed.

"Sounds great."

Twenty minutes later, I'd bought three books—including one by a local indigenous author—and I was quite pleased.

Demetrius had bought several LGBTQ young adult novels, a book about parenting queer teenagers, and a box set of three young-adult fantasy novels.

The Zaragosa trilogy was, apparently, written by a local university professor. Although she was on the shy side, she did regularly sign books.

Dickens explained that once Demetrius moved to town, he could bring the books in and Dickens would arrange to get them autographed.

My new friend was enchanted. Especially pleased at the idea of getting signed books. And, although Alaina was a little young, Dickens assured us the trilogy was good for all kids and hugely popular.

We each left with a cloth bag, emblazoned with the store's logo, and grins on our faces.

The sun had set and night was truly upon us.

"That was really nice of them." I met Demetrius's gaze.

"I want to say we bought enough to make it worth their while, but I doubt they'd see it that way."

"You got that feeling too, eh? Part of the community and happy to step up. Oh, I mentioned Pride Camp, and Dickens said he could arrange a discount for all the campers attending. He said he'd put together a card and either drop them off or I can come and get them."

"That's fantastic." Demetrius chuckled. "And Spike maintained he was just a mechanic while he helped me find well over a hundred bucks in fantastic books. Oh, I picked up one for Alaina about having a queer sibling. She's been so cool about everything, but I figured another book wouldn't hurt."

"You're such a good dad."

"I won't argue—although I'll readily admit I don't know everything. That I have so much to learn."

"Yeah." I glanced up at a streetlight. "I should be heading home."

"Oh. Let me drop off my books at the hotel, and then I'll walk you to your car."

"I'm okay to get there on my own." We were a block away from The Grand. Only five away from Stavros's.

"Still, I want to. I need a bit more exercise before bed."

"You shouldn't be winding down?" I never exercised this close to bedtime.

"A lovely stroll is hardly hardcore cardio." He winked. "Just give me one second."

"Sure."

We entered the lobby.

"Why don't you come up? You won't be able to see Baker, but you can see the beautifully renovated rooms."

I considered for a long time. *You should see the rooms. In case you need to recommend a reasonably priced hotel to one of the parents in the future.*

Sure. And for no other reason.

And yet I found myself smiling and saying, "Sure. Why not?"

Chapter Fourteen

Demetrius

T he room, which had felt spacious when I was alone, now seemed positively claustrophobic.

Still, as Jai moved to the window and pulled back the curtain, I couldn't help but admire him. His lithe body, his strong back, and his beautiful ass.

Over the years, when I thought about him, I'd remember two things—his puppy joy and his beautiful butt.

And now I knew why he'd disappeared. That made me so damn sad. And wanting to kill Gary the Gnat. What a monumental asshole.

I wasn't clear whether Gary had simply outed Jai or if he'd said something about the puppy persona. Either way, the guy was a class A fuckwit douchebag whose ass I would totally kick if we ever met. I wasn't a violent man, but every once in a while, I met someone who deserved a kick.

You would never.

Yeah...but I really want to.

"So you can see Baker from here?" Jai pointed in the direction of the volcano.

"Yeah. You kind of have to angle yourself because there's stuff between here and there...but yeah, you can see it. Just...stunning."

"My parents don't have a view. Just a ritzy house in an expensive part of town. Meant to show our family's wealth. I much preferred Arnav's home. So much happiness and laughter. Not austere. Not severe. Meant to show graciousness—not avarice."

I winced. "That wasn't any way to grow up."

"I certainly would never want that. For any child, let alone my own. I mean, I'm never going to have kids—"

"Why do you say that?" The question kind of burst out from my chest.

He closed the drapes, then turned back to me. "As you pointed out—I don't even have a home of my own. And although my salary is very generous, and I'm allowed to take on extra work during my off time, homes are still expensive. I've been working at camps—not exactly lucrative."

"Not like what you were doing before Gary the Gnat."

He blinked. "Who?"

"Your ex. I've decided he's Gary the Gnat."

"Oh." He frowned. "You know, I try really hard not to think of him at all. I mean, I loved my work at the camp back in Nova Scotia—very fulfilling. But I could've made a life volunteering out here. I shouldn't have had to go almost four thousand miles to outrun my demons."

Jesus.

"But you're back."

He pursed his lips. "Am I really? I haven't called my parents. Wouldn't be in touch with Arnav, if not for you. I certainly haven't contacted anyone from my old life..."

Your professional life, personal life, or pup life? I didn't ask.

"Well, you could do those things. Or you can move forward...which I think is what you're actually doing. Alessandra has given you a chance to start fresh. So you can make new friends—and keep the old ones worth keeping. You can confront your parents for their homophobia. Oh, I assume—"

He nodded.

"Right. So you can confront them or you can choose to ignore them. Live a good life, and you're already ahead of them."

"They..." He took a deep breath and let it out slowly. "I want to say they're just old school and old money, but they're bigoted and racist. Irony that someone in the minority would be racist, but they are. And terribly classist. I wish..." He ran his hands through his hair. "I wish Arnav's parents had been mine."

"Have you reconnected with them? Sounds like you were close to Arnav growing up. Did you have a relationship with his parents?"

"Yeah." He bit his lower lip. "I did. They were awesome—as were his older sisters. I didn't appreciate that at the time. I sure do now."

"So make the first move. Through Arnav or on your own. Just say you're back in town and wanting to reconnect. Something about knowing you might run into each other at the grocery store, but you want the first time to be more meaningful. Let them set the parameters. If they're anything like their son, I think you'll be welcomed with open arms." *God, please let me be right. But if they accepted a gay son, surely they'll accept his gay friend...*

"I could do that. I mean, I think I still have their number in my phone. Do people still have landlines?"

I chuckled. "Some older people do. I do. For emergencies. These days, though, if I was starting fresh, I'm not certain I would. Both my kids have cell phones. I thought Alaina might be too young, but she wants to go to and from school on her own. At eleven, she's earned that privilege. It's comforting to know she can get in touch with me if need be."

Jai advanced toward me. "I can see what a good dad you are. You have doubts. I think most good parents do. They worry about screwing up their kids. Parents who know what's best in all circumstances without hesitation...I find they're the ones who are often wrong. Life is a series of negotiations. You want what's best for your kids—but you're also willing to listen to their side of any argument."

I rubbed my hand. "I just want to do right by Erlene."

Slowly, telegraphing his movement, he grasped my hand. "I can tell you do. That you are. You're here, right? That says a lot about the kind of man you are. Many parents wouldn't have brought their kids to Pride Camp—let alone stayed close in a hotel to be nearby if anything bad happens."

"Like racoons."

"Like racoons." He smiled. "Vicious little shits."

"Uh, yeah." I squeezed his hand. "Watching Keegan have a hard time and not being able to do more than show up and insult racoons in support is so hard."

"I know." He squinted. "Okay, I don't *actually* know. I just see kids who are in pain and I want to solve all their problems. I can only imagine how their parents feel. Camp isn't just for kids—it's giving a respite to the parents as well. Vigilance takes a lot from a person. A few moments of peace can be worth a lot."

"I think you'd make a great parent. And before you argue, parenting comes in a lot of different forms. I essentially parented my sisters. As I said, I was eighteen, and they were fifteen when Nan died. I didn't see Erlene coming—and now I'm raising her two amazing kids. Arnav and Foster are looking into options of becoming parents. Aaron and

Noel—who I told you about—are looking into fostering options. And you've got your camp kids, if only for a short time."

"But I'm not working directly with them. I was before."

"Do you miss that part of it?"

"Sure—"

"Then find something similar in the offseason. Find a place to volunteer. There's got to be something in Mission City—some kid out there who needs guidance."

"You're right, of course." He met my gaze. "You seem to be often right."

I chuckled. "Running the odds. If I spout enough advice, something's bound to land."

"I think more lands than you realize."

"Well, that's the hope." A warmth spread through my chest at his shy smile.

Then something happened. His pupils widened, and he cocked his head. "I feel like..." He shook his head.

"Feel like...?"

"Like I know you. Which is ridiculous, because of course I know you."

Ah, recognition. Finally.

"You've been around for more than a week, and we've seen each other several times. We just spent three hours at a restaurant together. Best time I've had in a long time. A very long time."

Crap. Say something now or let it ride? Does it matter if he never puts the pieces together or will me broaching the subject make him feel more comfortable to be himself? Oh, what I wouldn't do for a crystal ball that would let me see into the future. "I had a good time as well. I'm glad you were able to relax."

Except I was anything but relaxed with him holding my hand.

"I want..." He swallowed.

"Want," I prompted.

"To kiss you."

Oh thank Christ. It's not just me. "That would be perfectly accept-able—thank you for asking."

He smiled that boyish smile that always dazzled me.

That still brought a hitch to my breathing. My pup was still in there. I was certain of it. Maybe someday I could help him find a new home. Somewhere secure and far away from harm.

He went up on tiptoes.

I bent my neck. My eyes drifted shut.

Our lips brushed.

As soft as I'd imagined.

He let go of my hand, grasped my cheeks, and tugged me closer. He opened his mouth and ran his tongue along the seam of my lips.

I opened for him on a sigh. A week of wanting. Six years of waiting. *Finally.*

I slid my hands down his sides then over the globes of his perfect ass. I squeezed.

He moaned.

I dragged him against me.

Our erect cocks brushed.

Yes. This. One hundred times this.

He pressed against me—trying to bring us as close together as possible.

I had no argument for this and melded our bodies together so I couldn't tell where he left off and where I began. My immediate reaction was to drag him to bed. Three things held me back. First—sup-plies. I didn't have condoms. He might...or I might be able to get some from the front desk...but that didn't feel right. Secondly—I worried he wasn't in the right headspace. We'd talked a lot about some pretty intense subjects tonight. I didn't want him hopping into bed with me to alleviate some of the pain I'd witnessed. Finally, I hadn't come clean with him. I'd yet to tell him I knew about his true self. But if he'd hung up his pup costume forever, he might not want that reminder. I was making excuses because I didn't want to drive Jai away, and bringing up the past might do just that. "Can I give you a blow job?"

He giggle-snorted. "Not where I expected this to go."

"Is that a yes?" A grin split my face.

He held my gaze. "Yeah, that would be...okay."

"Just okay?" I wanted to feign hurt, but he didn't always seem to get the joke.

"More than okay. But only if you want."

"I wouldn't have offered if I hadn't wanted to. I don't tend to do anything I don't want to." Unless it came to the kids. Sometimes I had to do what was right—not what I wanted.

"Uh, okay."

I pressed a kiss to the tip of his nose. Then, as graciously as I could, I sank to my knees. No easy feat—I was a big guy. But I'd done this a couple of times before. Not a lot, but enough to know what I was doing. Once I was as comfortable as I was going to get, I undid the button on his khakis. I slid the zipper down and then carefully pulled down both his pants and his boxer briefs.

His erection sprang free.

I licked my lips and gazed up at him.

He gently ran his hand across my short, curly hair. Then he offered a heartbreaking smile. Slowly, he nodded.

I grasped the base of his cock and brought the tip to my lips. I licked the slit, taking in the drop of precum.

"Oh, Jesus."

Fair. I planned to make him say a whole lot more than that before our time together was over. Slowly, I licked my way around his tip.

He swayed.

I pulled his crown into my mouth and swirled my tongue around him.

He let out a little groan.

Well okay, then. I sucked him in farther, continuing to run my tongue up and down his length. His taste was perfect. His scent was intoxicating. His little sounds of pleasure had me hardening further in my jeans. When I swallowed him down whole, nearly gagging, he jerked in me. I kept sucking and holding his thighs steady even as his breath stuttered.

He didn't give me a verbal warning, but his hands tightening against my scalp gave me enough of a hint of what was coming. He spurted into my mouth, and I continued to suck as I swallowed greedily.

"Demetrius..." He elongated the *s*.

My cock pressed painfully against my jeans.

His phone rang.

"Shit." He yanked out of my mouth with a pop, and drool dribbled down my chin.

As I still, somehow, had my wits about me, I found his phone in the back pocket of the khakis and handed it to him.

"Shit." He swiped. "Hey, Cody, what's up?"

Since I pegged the psychologist as a pretty responsible guy, this call worried me. Carefully, I pulled up Jai's boxer briefs and tucked him into them. Then I worked his pants up. *Wouldn't do for him to try to walk and then trip and hit his noggin.*

"Oh God. How are they?"

My ears perked as I zipped his pants and secured the button.

"You absolutely did the right thing in calling me. Are they headed to the Mission City or Abbotsford hospitals?" A pause. "I'm glad they're going to Abbotsford. Bigger hospital and more staff. All that's good but..." Another pause. "You've called their parents? Right, up north. I forgot."

Ah. Chris. At least *they* meant just one person and not a group, although by Jai's rigid demeanor—and the fact a camper was on their way to the hospital—this couldn't be good.

My erection, now waning, was no impediment to me standing—although I used the bed to rise faster. A bit of a head rush, but nothing I couldn't handle.

"I'm in downtown Mission City right now. I'll head to the Abbotsford hospital. All good." Another pause. "You did the right thing, Cody. Sounds like you worked as a team. I'll text—" He frowned. "Oh, of course you want to be there. If Grey and Makenna can watch—" More brow furrowing. "Right. I'll see you shortly." He ran his hand through his hair. "Good work." Then he stabbed the phone—clearly to disconnect the call.

"Fuck. Fuck. Fuck. Oh God, I'm going to be fired. And I shouldn't even be worrying about that because Chris is in an ambulance on the way to the hospital and I need to get there. My car! Jesus. I can run. I need to go. Like, right now."

"Jai." I needed to calm him, because him taking off in this state wasn't going to help. Yes, he needed to get to the hospital. Him crashing his SUV on the way wasn't going to help anyone—least of all Chris.

"You don't understand. I should've been there tonight. I never should have left. If something happens—"

"Jai." Again, calm and authoritative. Like when Keegan was spiraling.

"Their life was in danger. I might've prevented what happened. I mean, if something happens—"

"Jai."

Still with the wild hand gestures, as if beseeching me to understand.

I did. If Keegan had been hurt, I'd be beside myself. But my mind worked differently than Jai's clearly did. Bad things helped me focus on the essential and block out all the noise. I'd deal with the crisis and push all the noise—including self-recriminations—to the background.

Jai was obviously the opposite. Panic was sending his mind skittering all over the place and obviously nothing I said was going to calm him.

So I did the only thing I knew to do. "Stop! Sit!"

He plopped his ass onto the bed.

I took a short-lived breath of relief.

Chapter Fifteen

Jai

*D*id he just...? And did I...? Wow. Even as I tried to absorb what was happening, my mind settled.

"Good boy, Buttercup. You're a good boy."

Demetrius was crooning to me. I was seated on the bed in his hotel room, and he was standing before me, hands on his knees, and his gaze level with mine.

"My Buttercup is a good boy. You're going to breathe slowly."

My mind wanted to rebel—because I had something super important to do. But his words settled something within me. Something long-forgotten. I blinked. "Big D?"

A grin broke out across his face. "You remember. You were always my favorite. Now—may I pet you?"

I bobbed my head quickly. I wanted his touch. Craved his touch. His touch always soothed.

He eased himself onto the bed next to me and gathered me into his arms. He feathered my hair with one hand while giving me scritches up and down my back with the other. His familiarity overwhelmed me. Memories of six years ago flooded me.

How did I not recognize him from the beginning? This is Big D. D. Demetrius. Also Big Daddy.

Because I'd been in a monogamous relationship with Gary, I hadn't engaged in any kind of sex acts with anyone. For me, What'sUp Pup was playtime. Scritches and ball chasing and puppy piles. Big D used to bring me treats and chew toys and— "You left me those treats. And that toy." My voice was barely above a whisper.

"I did, pup. I hoped you'd remember me."

"I didn't...but I do now."

"That's good. And we're going to talk about this later. Right now, though, I need to drive you to the Abbotsford Hospital. You need to make sure Chris is okay."

My mind coalesced around his words, and I tensed.

"It's okay, pup. I'll be there for you."

"I should drive."

"You might be calmer now, but you're still not in any shape to drive. I can stay in the car, if you want, but I'm taking you." He pressed a kiss to my temple. "Are you ready to go?"

"Uh, yeah." My head still felt a little woozy, but clarity was coming. The panic was receding. It had been a very long time since I'd lost my shit so badly like that.

About six years, to be precise.

I wasn't prone to panic. Stress and anxiety? Sure. Pure panic? Rarely.

With Demetrius's help, I rose to my feet. "Thank you."

"Let's get you to the hospital first. Then you can thank me." He yanked his keys out of his pocket. The he grasped me under the elbow and steered me toward the door.

Within two minutes we were down the elevator and heading toward his minivan. Less than two minutes after that, he selected the Abbotsford Hospital on his GPS and headed out, following the directions. He was instructed to drive south as Abbotsford was that way—across the Mission-Abby bridge.

I probably could've directed him, but I was busy sending a flurry of texts as we drove over the brightly lit bridge. That, and I hadn't been there in, like, fifteen years. I'd been a healthy kid and not prone to doing stupid shit that would land me in the hospital. "I've let Smith know."

"Not Alessandra?"

"She tends to go to bed earlier because Wesley's an early riser. Smith is still a night owl, and he deals with the baby if he wakes." I continued typing. "I've told him I can handle things—"

"Which you can."

"—but that I'd keep him informed." I took a deep breath.

Demetrius followed the directions down a highway that had farm fields on either side. "What happened?"

"Huh?" I rubbed my forehead.

"What happened to Chris?" He glanced at me quickly before refocusing on the road. "I mean, if you can't tell me..."

"Somehow they got stung by something. A bee or wasp or something. They're allergic—which we knew—and they had a bad reaction. Grey administered their EpiPen, which worked..."

"But the patient always needs to be seen by a doctor."

"Yeah." I ran my hand through my hair. "I should have—"

"Stop." Hard. But not as harsh as before. "Take a breath."

"You don't have to boss me around." With a tinge of defensiveness. *Although you deserve this. You sat when he ordered you to. You obeyed that command without a second thought. You recognized him instantly. No more masks. No more hiding from your past.*

"Buttercup, I know I don't. I'm not your Daddy. But I'm someone who is very worried about you. If you show up at the hospital panicking, that's not going to help anyone. Chris is in good hands. They'll take care of them."

"Chris..." I let out a long breath. "I can't get into specifics, but Chris has had negative interactions with medical authorities before."

"Ah."

Hopefully he understood. Trans and nonbinary kids had a rough enough time in life without having to deal with people who might not be empathetic.

My phone buzzed and I checked the screen, taking in the words quickly. "Makenna says the campers are hunkered down and watching a movie in the great room."

"You can send word back once you've seen Chris. Damn, do you have authority?"

"Yes. Cody's bringing the paperwork. I have a copy on my phone as well. Their parents are up north and wouldn't be able to get here."

"Are you going to call them?" He chanced another glance at me.

I bit my lower lip. "I will, of course. But I might as well wait until I have a firm grasp of what's happening. If it's serious and they need to come, an extra hour out of the loop won't make a difference. If Chris is going to be okay, then better to give them that news."

He shrugged. "I'd want to know. I wouldn't be able to get to Alaina...but I'd still want to know." He pursed his lips. "But I respect you know what you're doing."

Except I didn't. I just didn't see how dragging people out of bed in the middle of the night was going to solve anything. Was I right or wrong? An hour wouldn't likely make a difference—but if we waited until the picture was clearer, it would give the family enough information to know if they had to rush home or if Chris was going to be okay.

As we came into a more populated area of the town, the GPS directed us to turn several times. Demetrius followed the instructions as I continued to work my phone.

"I'll drop you off at the Emergency entrance and go park. Do you want me to come in?" His deep voice soothed me.

The GPS directed this last turn onto the street with the hospital.

"You might as well come in. No point staying in the car." I checked for messages one final time, then watched as he turned right.

"Well, if Cody's driving, you could get a ride back to your SUV with him."

"Oh." Well, that was something I hadn't considered. "But Cody's going to know someone brought me. If he asks, I can't lie."

"I wouldn't ask you to. But he might not inquire."

My wry laughter filled the minivan. "There's no way Cody's not going to ask me how I got here. He's whip-smart. He's one of those people who can take in dozens of data points at once and sort them quickly. I'm someone who can only handle a couple at a time, and it takes me a long time to make a decision. Great for a financial ana-lyst—not so much for handling crises."

"Okay first, that's kind of bullshit. You process things differently, and I'm quite certain you're normally great in a crisis."

Silence. I had no way to answer that.

"The circumstances tonight were what threw you off. If you'd been at the camp, you would've done things brilliantly. I doubt you worked in Nova Scotia for five years and nothing ever went wrong."

"It did." A tad defensive.

"You were off your game." He signaled to turn into the entrance to the hospital. "You'd just had an orgasm."

"Jesus, do you have to be so blunt?"

"Jai, I've always been this blunt. I'm just saying you need to cut yourself some slack. You're not Cody. He's not you. Chris is lucky both of you will be here. Oh, there's the entrance." He pulled to the spot closest to the massive emergency sign. "Now, I can head back—"

"Please come in."

"Okay. I'll see you in a couple of minutes."

I hopped out and strode into the emergency room, ready to deal with whatever was coming next.

Chapter Sixteen

Demetrius

Taking a deep breath, I scoped out the closest parking space. Within a couple of minutes, I was at the machine entering my license plate number and tapping my credit card. On impulse, I paid for twelve hours. If I didn't use it, that was okay. Basically, the money would go to the hospital anyway, which was good for them. I could afford the usurious amount required just to give my beloved minivan a spot.

When I entered the ER, I was prepared to go to the front desk, but Cody approached me.

"Jai said you'd be coming. He's showing the paperwork to the administrator. Hopefully that will get him in with Chris."

I nodded.

He pointed to a couple of empty chairs, and we moved to them.

"How is Chris?" I winced. "Sorry, none of my business."

"I can tell you they were okay when the ambulance took them away. The epinephrine worked. But they needed to get checked out."

"Sure."

Cody winced. "But the paramedics weren't happy with nonbinary."

"Yeah."

"I only arrived a couple of minutes before you, and I've been trying to explain to anyone who would listen about Chris, but I wasn't getting anywhere."

I sighed. "I'm sorry to hear that."

"Well, Jai's got medical authority, so that should help." He gazed at me.

"He told me all this, and I promise you that I'll never say anything. I've run up against resistance from the system before. Keegan being gay is tough enough—I can't imagine how parents of trans and nonbinary kids cope."

"The best they can in a structure not designed for them." Cody rubbed his eyes. "I do my best to help them navigate the system, but I'm not a medical professional. Hell, my mentor, Kennedy, has been doing this a lot longer than I have, and she still struggles. Oh hell." He yanked out his phone. "Max Crawford is a psychiatrist who sees patients at the ranch. He might be able to help. I'll text Kennedy."

I glanced at the clock on the wall. Well past ten. I almost suggested he not bother Kennedy. *Yeah, but if you could do something to help someone, you'd want to be asked. If you had the ability, you'd do it.*

"Damn." Cody stared at his screen. "Max is at a conference in Toronto. He has privileges with the hospital, but it's almost two in the morning there. Kennedy asked if I want her to come." He met my gaze. "I think we're doing okay."

"We are. Jai has the paperwork. Kennedy being here...would she be able to influence things?" I wracked my brain to try to remember Kennedy's connection.

"Not likely. She's a psychologist, like myself, no MD privileges. Only she's been at this a lot longer than I have." His phone pinged. "She's offered…" He typed furiously. "Okay. I told her we had things under control." He met my gaze.

"We do. If Jai needs help, he'll ask. You've got Kennedy on speed dial."

"Right." He rubbed his eyes again. Then, as if for the first time, he really looked at me.

Yep. Here it comes.

"Nice of you to drive Jai here. At least I'm assuming—"

"I drove him here."

"Ah."

Might as well lay things on the line. "We had dinner. Turns out we knew each other back in Vancouver. Well, Jai didn't remember right away, but I did. As friends, we went out to dinner."

"Right."

Like I told Jai…this kid's pretty swift.

Wait, he's twenty-six and a psychologist…so not a kid.

"We ate at Stavros's and then wandered down First Avenue."

"Lovely walk."

"Yes. We went into The Owl's Nest. Do you know Dickens and Spike?"

Cody arched an eyebrow—as if trying to decide whether to let me steer the conversation away from the personal or not. "I know Dickens and I've met Spike. He's a good mechanic. If I ever get a motorcycle, he'll be the one I see."

"Are you planning to get a bike?"

"Nope. My mom would kill me before I even had a chance to be in an accident." He shrugged. "You?"

"I tried. I really did. I struggled to ride a bike as a kid, and the motorcycle was just as frustrating. My brain just isn't wired that way."

"Really? I'll admit I've never heard that before."

"Well, then I married Erlene and figured I needed to be safe. I bought a used minivan and have never looked back. Would I love to ride with the wind in my hair? Sure."

Cody burst out laughing as I rubbed my nearly shorn head. "Good one."

"I try."

"I bet if you asked Spike, he'd take you out for a spin. He might even have one of those sidecar things."

My eyes bugged.

Cody laughed again. "The look on your face—"

"Can you see me in a sidecar?"

"While holding Dickens's cat Ari who would be wearing goggles? Absolutely. I'd pay good money to see that."

I'd met the rather rotund cat, Aristotle. Quite a charmer, she was. I wasn't really a cat person, but I'd found myself enchanted by her.

Jai heading our way caught my eye, and I rose.

As did Cody.

Jai offered a small smile. "They're resting. The doctors want them to stay the night. Chris asked if I could stay as well, which I will."

I nodded. "How about I run to Timmies and grab you a coffee? And maybe a dozen donuts for the staff?"

"Yeah, that would be a great idea."

Cody gazed between the two of us. "I can come back in the morning to pick you and Chris up. Or do you want us to bring your SUV here? Demetrius and I would be happy to do it."

I appreciated Cody's understanding I just wanted to help.

"Would you mind?"

"Not at all." I smiled. "I'll drive Cody now. He'll drive your SUV here, and then he'll be able to drive his car back to camp."

"Or I can drive Demetrius. Do you have a preference for who drives your SUV?"

Jai met my gaze. "Would you mind doing it? Then Cody can get back to the camp sooner."

"Of course." I offered a smile. "I'll do the Timmie's run on the way back."

"There's a 24 hour one just down the road. I'll show you." Cody held my gaze. "I'll be out front when you're ready." He nodded to Jai and then headed out.

We stood for a good thirty seconds just gazing at each other.

"I can't…"

"I don't expect you to." I resisted the urge to take his hand. "You've got a lot going on. You've got my number. Don't be a stranger, okay?"

"Yeah."

"Do you need a hug?"

"Yeah."

"Well, that I can do." I pulled him into my arms, tucking his head under my chin. "You'll be okay. Everything's going to be okay."

"You're right. I spoke to Chris's family. Chris assured them that they were fine, and they didn't need family swooping down and taking over."

"Ah."

"Chris's dad had to be talked down, but their mother made a sound and reasonable case why they wouldn't be able to do anything anyway and since they were on vacation, why not stay? She said they'd come if Chris wanted them to. In the end, Chris didn't."

"Brave."

"Pragmatic. It would cost thousands to book new flights. The doctors have assured us that Chris is out of danger. It's not their parents' first round with an EpiPen event, so they know the drill. Chris will be back at camp before they could get here. And you need to go. Cody's waiting."

"You're a good man, Jai."

He pulled back to meet my gaze. "I do my best. I will be in touch—I promise."

I let him go.

He headed back to Chris.

I headed into the dark night of the unknown.

Chapter Seventeen

Jai

S omehow, I managed to get Chris back to camp in time for break-fast. They ate voraciously, accepted the well-wishes from every-one, and then went to their room to crash.

I did much the same thing—having slept little at the hospital. I woke in time for lunch and found it delivered with a knock on my door by Cody.

Crap. "Hey, come on in."

He grinned, handing me a paper bag. "Chef made it special for you."

I was almost afraid to ask because I had never given my preferences to our eerily omniscient head of *making everyone healthy while in-dulging them* person.

We sat at the table.

Cody yanked out his cold cuts sub and grinned.

I pulled out my peanut-butter-and-banana sandwich and smiled, despite myself. "My best friend's mom used to make these for me when I went over. A decidedly non-Indian food. How did Chef know?"

"I honestly have no clue." He slid off his chair and headed to the cupboards. "I'm thinking water is in order."

"With peanut butter? Absolutely. Better with milk."

"Oh." Cody's eyes lit as he detoured to the fridge. Moments later, he was back with two glasses.

"I could've come to the great hall."

"You look like shit."

I blinked.

"Just keeping it real." He sipped his milk. "Chris had lunch and is working with the group on their play. They're a hell of a writer. I suspect they'll go to bed early tonight, but I don't see any lingering effects—psychological or physical."

"That's a relief." I poked my bag. "Chips?"

Cody shrugged. "We're allowed." He eyed his sandwich. "So, you and Mr. Fulton...?"

I winced.

"He said you were just friends."

"We are friends."

"He said you knew each other from *before*."

"He did?"

"No specifics." Cody held my gaze. "I'm not just here for the kids."

"I can't..."

"Then call Kennedy. Because something's going on. It's not affecting your work, but I see it."

Crap. "Something happened a couple of days ago, and I didn't connect the dots. Now I have." *Demetrius left me the treats. He did it to tease, not to threaten. He just didn't realize it would have the opposite effect.*

"I still think…" He toyed with his sandwich. "I don't know much about your history."

"Right." *Because you're my employee. I'm the boss.*

"But…"

"Oh dear. Nothing good ever starts with *but*."

He smiled. "I could make a crass joke—"

"Oh God, I walked right into that one."

"You did." He winked. "But you're making a good point."

So was he.

"I'll talk to Kennedy. If she has time—"

"She'll be here at four." He bit into his sandwich.

"You little interfering shit."

He shrugged, chewed vigorously, then swallowed. Then gulped some milk. "I didn't time that well. She's coming to check in with me. But I figure if you took her on a tour—"

"She's been on a tour."

"But not recently. Certainly not with the campers here." Again, he shrugged. "You can tell her everything or nothing. I'm not in a position to counsel you. Explicit rules about dating parents aren't in the handbook. Or at least not in mine—"

"Mine either. They probably never envisioned this."

"Well, it's not like you showing one camper preferential treatment would really make any difference."

"It's the perception."

"True. Well, camp's over in a week. You'll just have to decide what happens between now and then. Or after…if the family moves to Mission City."

Which was the thought that carried me right up until Kennedy's visit.

Firstly, she brought the ranch's therapy dog Tiffany. Said yellow lab allowed herself to be fawned over by the admiring crowd.

"Why don't you give me the tour? Cody can handle Tiffany." Kennedy grinned.

"Your dog appears quite capable of handling herself." I grinned right back.

"That she is. She's been doing this for a while."

We headed from the great hall outside.

Kennedy slid her sunglasses on, hiding those fathomless and incisive brown eyes. Her long, chestnut-colored hair flowed down her back, and she looked very casual in her jeans and T-shirt. She might be a psychologist, but her practice was on a horse-therapy ranch. "Cody says you want to show me around." She grinned.

"Cody's got a big mouth." I groused.

She laughed. "I want to say he's worried about you—which he is—but he's not going to show that or tell me. I just...I've known him for years. With his patients, he can sort of hold things in—at least in front of them. With me? He tends to be more open."

Which echoed what I'd witnessed. He was easygoing, and the campers shared quite freely with him—but he was guarded about how much of himself he gave away.

"After we're done talking here, I'm going to offer him a spot on my roster at the ranch—if he's interested. We never have enough counselors. Rainbow and I have found a way to configure another counseling office, so he'd have his own space. And don't worry, I'm not poaching him. He'll always be free to return here if he wants to. We're flexible."

Rainbow, Kennedy's younger sister, was the ranch manager and, according to Kennedy, held the place together. Healing Horses Ranch had a stellar reputation as one of the best counseling centers in all of Cedar Valley

"It's an amazing opportunity."

"One I want him to take his time considering. It's not unheard of for a patient to return to their counseling center as a therapist—but it's still a mind shift. Something I'm certain he's capable of."

"He wouldn't be the only queer counselor."

"Right. I've had Justin working with me for a few years now. He's doing his PhD out of Simon Fraser. He and Cody get along so damn well. And not just because they're both gay. Cody's still a kid at heart, and he's so good with Angus and Opal, Justin and Stanley's two young ones. I've got Denise Lang as the child psychologist, but she wants to focus on younger kids. Cody tackling youth just works. And he'll likely have adult clients as well—we're all flexible."

"You work a lot." We'd arrived at the beach.

"It's a vocation, Jai. A calling. I knew from the time I was little and putting my sisters into *counseling* that I was meant to do this."

"Your seven sisters." I rubbed the back of my neck. "I can't even fathom that."

"The infamous Dixon sisters. Didn't you go to school with one of us?"

"Sunshine."

Kennedy laughed. "Oh, to have been a fly on the proverbial wall." She grinned. "Have you seen Sunshine since you've been back?"

I shook my head.

"Well, you should drop in to The Owl's Nest."

I snapped my fingers. "I was there yesterday." *God, was it really just yesterday? And shit...I left the books for Wesley in Demetrius's room...*

"And you saw Dickens?"

"Yeah, with his husband, Spike. Really nice guys."

"They are. Dickens adores Sunshine, even though he acts put upon by her."

"She is…a handful."

Another chuckle. "That she is. If you haven't heard already, she's got two divorces behind her. I'm hopeful she'll meet the right person."

"Protective older sister?"

She nodded. "I thought her first marriage was a good one, but life intervened. I knew the second one was a disaster before the vows and, unfortunately, I wasn't proven wrong. Still, she's the most optimistic of us. And we're not talking about what's important to you."

I gazed at the water lapping the sandy shore. "Cody's got a big mouth."

"I would take issue with that. He's good at keeping secrets." She brushed a flyaway lock of hair from her face. "He's just worried about you. Sounds like last night was rough."

"And I turned up at the hospital with a parent."

"Well, yeah." She was nearly my height, so when our gazes met, we were on the same level. "And if you tell me that it's none of my business, I'll respect that."

She would. I had no doubt. She was also giving me the chance to share—if I could find the courage. "We weren't on a date. Or at least that wasn't how it started out. He convinced me to have dinner with him—as a friend."

"Okay."

"I know this is going to sound a little…questionable. I felt safe with him. Like I knew him or something which, it turns out, I did. Or do. Or…" I ran my hand through my hair. "I didn't recognize him…but was drawn to his…energy? Is that the right word?"

"Well, yes. I'm also incredibly curious how you didn't recognize him. Again, none of my business."

"Dark club, out of context..." *Masks.*

"Ah. That's fair. I had a few ideas in mind, and I'll admit that wasn't one of them." She grinned. "Okay...energy."

"I didn't intend for things to..."

"You're worried about implicating him."

"Yeah."

"I'll reiterate this stays between us. And you only share what you're comfortable with. We might not be in my office—but this space is just as sacred."

Right. Which I'd known. Having it spelled out really helped. So did the gentle lapping of the lake against the shore in the light breeze. "I'm gay." I held her gaze, even though I couldn't see her eyes behind her dark glasses. "Which you'd probably already figured out."

"I don't make assumptions, Jai. And Cody didn't provide a gender for the parent."

"One of the dads. A great guy, and once I remembered...well, everything came back about that time—the good, the bad, the horrifically ugly... But I had the ill camper to get to. I really panicked."

"Understandable. You feel responsible for these teenagers. That's a lot to take on."

"I felt guilty about having taken a night off."

"I can see that. And I can suggest you're not obliged to be monitoring the kids twenty-four hours a day. Cody, Grey, and Makenna all get time off. A dinner away wasn't unreasonable."

"Yes, but look what happened." Panic again rose within me.

"Can you not admit it likely would've happened anyway?"

"Probably." I gazed down at my running shoes. "But that's not the point."

"Could you have done anything better than what Cody did in that moment?"

"Well, no."

"Do Smith or Alessandra blame you?"

"Not at all."

"See?"

"But they only know I was out...not who I was with."

"Ah." She gazed skyward just as an eagle flew across the lake. "You think they'll be upset?"

"I think I would be, if I were in their shoes."

"And do you want to see the parent again? As more than a friend?"

"Uh..." I bit my lip. "I have nothing but incredibly fond memories of him. Would we be able to rekindle that relationship? I honestly don't know. But I'm not going to risk the way things are now just for a shot."

"A shot? At happiness?" She arched an eyebrow. "Life is full of regrets and missed connections. Maybe this is one worth taking." She shrugged. "But that's up to you. Let's go back, eh?"

We walked back in silence as I mulled over her words.

Regardless of my decision, I had to come clean with Alessandra and Smith.

Chapter Eighteen

Demetrius

"You texted your sister about moving?" I sat across from Keegan and Cody in the latter's office. The bright-blue paint reminded me of the lake, and the painted forest scene could've felt juvenile—except it didn't. The entire room reflected the nature just outside the windows.

"You didn't say I couldn't." Keegan held my stare.

For about ten seconds.

Then he looked away.

"Sure...but..." I gazed beseechingly at Cody.

Who offered a sympathetic smile. "I think what your dad is trying to say, Keegan, is that he would've preferred to speak to your sister first."

I nodded. "She was supposed to be out of touch for another two days." I thought I had two days to figure out what to say. How to broach this subject.

Well, I actually thought I had six days because I'd wanted to do this in person. More fool me for thinking Keegan wouldn't jump the gun.

He raised his chin. "I just wanted to find out what she thought. I didn't say we *were* moving here."

"Maybe not."

Memories of Alaina's call returned to me with full force. Her *oh God, this is the best news ever* still ringing in my ear.

"I still believe it should've come from me. I am, supposedly, the adult in this relationship."

Both Cody and Keegan smiled.

Undoubtedly for different reasons.

"Dad..." Keegan sighed. "I just wanted to ask her what she thought."

"You attempted to influence her."

He shook his head vigorously. "I didn't. I swear. I just said she'd be near Glynnis and wouldn't that be awesome?"

"She's eleven, Keegan. Of course being near her best friend would be *awesome.* But there are serious issues that I, as the adult, need to work out. It's not as simple as packing a bag and moving fifty miles."

"Dad..." Keegan gave me what I thought of as his puppy-dog eyes. Something I was entirely powerless to ignore—try as I might.

"Yes?"

"I know there is grown-up stuff. Like where will we live and which school will we go to and..." He flailed his arms.

"Selling the old condo, arranging school records, finding extra-curricular programs Alaina will like, figuring out if moving to the Bible Belt of Cedar Valley is really the best thing for you." I eyed Cody.

He smiled. "Life isn't perfect anywhere. And just because Cedar Valley—and Mission City—has plenty of religious folk"—his smile didn't waver—"of all faiths, I might add, doesn't mean LGBTQ people aren't as safe as in Vancouver. There are bigots everywhere."

"And bullies." Keegan raised his chin—daring me to argue.

"Vancouver has more resources."

"Cody says I can keep seeing him. That there's a group of kids at the high school who are queer or queer-friendly. There are a lot of good things here." He blinked. "I like the friends I've made. You can work from anywhere—"

"Keegan."

"Well, it's true." He plowed past my warning tone. "You were great—staying home when we needed you."

I'd left a good-paying government job with stability, benefits, and a pension, for a more flexible job in the private sector. In this case, I'd taken a pay cut. "I did what I had to do. Zero regrets. I hope you know that."

He nodded. "So maybe, if things settle with me, you could do something else—if you wanted to. Alaina and I don't need babysitting anymore."

"You'll be in high school while she's finishing middle school. And there's the matter of your French studies..." Erlene had registered both kids in French Immersion. And, according to their teachers, both excelled. If they could stay in their programs until they completed high school, they would be considered officially bilingual. That would open worlds for them—including government jobs.

I, on the other hand, had barely spoken two words of the language before I'd become friends with Erlene. The day I'd met the kids—and seen their homework—I'd bought an app and started studying fifteen minutes a day. In all these years, no matter how chaotic life had been, I'd never missed a day. Last thing before I went to bed. Even the day Erlene died and her funeral. I just had to repeat to myself, over and over, that I was doing it for the kids. And after all this time? My spoken wasn't great, but I could at least understand some of their homework...

"The Mission City high school has a French Immersion program, and I know several of the French Immersion teachers at Cedar Street Elementary. I even went to school with one of them—Felix Stevenson. Great guy. Loves kids. Newly married. To Jacob." Cody met, and held, my gaze.

More gay folks. More people I could connect with. More members of the community who would, quite probably, support my son. "I'll...take all this under consideration."

Keegan pumped his fist.

"I haven't made a decision." I attempted to keep my voice stern.

Cody covered his mouth—and likely his smile—with a hand.

Keegan jumped to his feet and came over to me.

I rose quickly and caught him in a big hug. *My little boy's growing up. If he can face change, maybe I need to as well.*

Alaina had texted me with a flurry of exclamation points and emojis—letting me know how damn excited she was. I had sent back a gently worded text. First asking if she was okay—given she wasn't supposed to have cell service—and secondly cautioning her nothing had been determined.

My message had gone unread, and I hadn't heard back.

Her friend Shanice's mom was driving them back from the island on Monday and dropping her off.

Cody rose as well. "Give me a couple of minutes with your dad?"

Keegan nodded. "Yeah, that would be okay." His gaze shot between the two of us. "But you're going to talk him into it, right?"

The psychologist smiled. "We're going to have an adult conversation."

My boy pursed his lips.

I placed my hand on his shoulder and guided him to the door. "I promise to keep an open mind."

To my surprise, he gave me another hug. "I love you." He whispered the words fiercely under his breath.

Then he was gone.

I pivoted back to Cody. "So tell me what you really think."

And the psychologist did.

Thirty minutes later, I wandered outside, still in a bit of a daze. *Am I really considering this? What does it mean for the kids? For me?* I spied a picnic table and headed that way. No campers were in sight. In fact, I was completely alone. I plopped down, yanked out my phone, and checked to see if I had any messages from Alaina.

Nothing.

"May I sit with you?" A woman's soft voice pulled me from my contemplations.

I glanced up to see Alessandra MacLean. The patron saint of the camp. Her idea and her family's money had made Pride Camp a reality. "Uh, sure."

She sat across from me. "I'm taking a break from everything—social worker, mother, wife...even camp...whatever I am. I'm just being Allie for a few minutes."

"Oh." *Am I supposed to know what to say? I wish I wasn't such a dork when it came to some interactions.* Anything to do with the kids? I was intelligent and articulate. Life in general? Not so much.

"You son is a lovely young man."

"Yeah, Keegan's great. Thank Hamish again for me, please, for recommending this place."

"Hamish is a great employee and able to build bridges. I'm lucky to have him working for me at the EAP company. He's dedicated to community service. Pretty much all of my employees are."

"That's awesome." I'd had access to employee assistance programs before, but had never availed myself of their services. Until my life started spinning out of control with Keegan being bullied.

"How are you doing? Missing Keegan in your daily life? I remember you saying your daughter was away from home for the first time as well."

"Great memory."

She shrugged one shoulder as if to deflect the compliment.

"Yes, Alaina's hiking on Vancouver Island. Keegan hasn't been apart from me before either. I'm a bit of a protective papa bear."

"I can see how much you love them. Much as my mother loved me. I lost my father when I was young—to an industrial accident."

"So you know about losing a parent."

Allie nodded. "Just me and my mom. I was gutted when she died a few years ago. She never got to meet her grandchild or see the mansion I live in." She rolled her eyes. "It's a little much—but Smith's right in that we need a level of security."

I didn't know how to answer. The threats in our family's lives were the psychological ones made by Keegan's bullies. "Yeah. Right."

She turned her gaze to me. "I understand you helped us the other night."

I cocked my head.

"You drove Jai to the hospital and then ensured he had his vehicle. That was helpful. Smith offered to come down, but Jai said he had things under control."

"He did."

"I know." She offered an enigmatic smile.

Or what I saw as such.

"Jai spoke to me. About you."

"Oh?" *Shit, shit, shit.*

"I won't speak out of school, but he clearly likes you. A lot."

"Well, I like him too."

"Having a parent date an administrator isn't really aboveboard."

"I know, ma'am. Jai has scruples." *Except when his cock was in my mouth.*

Probably the wrong thought.

"We can't control, sometimes, how we feel about people. My husband and I had a very rocky start to our relationship. Took us a long time to find our footing. And it's Allie. Not ma'am. That's...not me."

I offered a grin. "Okay, I can sort of see that about you."

"I'm all for forthrightness. Smith and I had a long conversation with Jai. Once camp is over, he's free to see whomever he wants. We're just asking for you to hold off another five days."

"That's fair." *Except I'm going back to Vancouver. Maybe forever.*

"Look...I'm friends with Paisley's parents. She and her brother are coming to stay with us for a couple of days after camp's over. Their parents got a chance for a Caribbean cruise at the last minute. Personally, I'm not going anywhere that hot in the middle of July, but I'm all about helping out. Since Keegan and Paisley are close, I was wondering if he might want to stay with us for a night as well? Perhaps we can meet your daughter as well? She's welcome to stay as well. Kyle, Paisley's brother, is her age and he's wicked with pickle ball."

"Alaina loves pickle ball."

"So Keegan was saying. Smith had a court installed last year." Allie smiled. "Look, I know inviting your kid to stay at our place is a little unorthodox."

"Yeah." In truth, my first instinct was to say no. To hold them closer to me as we navigated these new, and treacherous, waters.

But I also needed to spend some alone time with Jai.

Alaina came first, so the choice would be hers. "Maybe we can play it by ear?"

"Of course. Smith and I don't have a ton of experience with older children. Now, this would be contingent on your two liking toddlers—"

"They love toddlers. Truly. My neighbor has a little girl, and Keegan babysits. He's young, I know, but totally responsible. I'm always next door." Because I didn't want her to think I wasn't a responsible parent.

She waved me off. "I was babysitting at twelve so I could save money for university. I completely understand."

"Alaina likes to hold the baby and talk about being a mother. That terrifies me. In the next breath, though, she'll say that's after she visits the moon while piloting a space vehicle. Oh, and I can't forget how she's going to cure cancer." I held Allie's gaze. "She's so damn smart. Keegan is as well, don't get me wrong. But Alaina...?"

"I can't wait to meet her."

"You would just let four kids stay overnight in your house?"

"I can provide a list of references for us—"

"I'm not saying that. I mean I'm glad you're not, as far as I can tell, monsters."

"We're not."

"But then why?"

"Practice."

"I want to call BS."

She raised an eyebrow as the corners of her lips curled. "I'm cock-blocking you right now. For the protection of the campers and the reputation of the camp. Propriety and all that bullshit." Her grin widened. "But after? I think you and Jai need some time to talk. He can go to Vancouver, of course. Or you can leave the kids in Vancouver and come here."

"I don't want to do that."

"Hence bringing them to our place. We have plenty of guest rooms. Eventually one will be Wesley's bedroom as we're hoping, if we're blessed, to have another child. And given how challenging this one has been, I might need my head examined for wanting more."

"Only-children survive. But my sisters were my reason for living when I lost first Mom and then Nan."

"You were lucky to have them."

"They're the bane of my existence and one of my greatest joys."

"You're a good man, Demetrius."

I blinked. "You barely know me."

"Perhaps." She gestured around the camp. "You're here. You care—"

"I'm considering moving to Mission City."

She cocked her head.

"Keegan really likes it here. He thinks...I dunno...that life will be different here. I keep saying this, but he wants a fresh start. Now he's got Alaina on board, and suddenly I'm the one who's holding everyone back."

"You're the rational adult." Said with no small amount of amusement.

"Right?" I scratched my chin. "Everyone seems to forget that."

She regarded me. "I'm not going to go into details about my life—it's a little boring...but also very personal. I needed a fresh start. I had a rough go of it for a while, and I had to find a way to move forward. Smith gave me the push. He was also there to catch me—in case I tripped and fell."

"But you didn't."

"Nope. I built a life for myself that I could be proud of. I did some pretty crappy things during my dark period. Unlike you. You've held your family together and put your children first."

Did I tell Hamish all this? Did Jai tell her? Or is she intuiting this? Because she's not wrong... "Uh, yeah. Of course I put the kids first."

"Right. So maybe it's time for you to put yourself first. If you're not interested in Jai as more than a friend, that's okay. Even friends, though, deserve some time without kids around." After clear hesitation, she placed her hand over mine. "Just think about it." She squeezed my hand, then stood, released me, and headed off toward Jai's cabin.

I had a lot to think about.

Chapter Nineteen

Jai

S tanding in the deserted campground, my sadness warred with excitement.

The campers had gone home four days ago.

Grey and Makenna had left soon after the debrief with Cody, Alessandra, Smith, and me.

Cody had accepted Kennedy's offer of employment as a psychologist at her therapy ranch and was arranging his schedule.

I'd spent the past three days preparing everything for the session starting in just over a week for the older campers.

Makenna and Grey would be back then as well.

Tonight, though, I was alone. In fact, I was going to be alone up here most of the time.

Alessandra had fretted over that—until I pointed out having someone on site, especially during the summer, made sense. We had a gate I locked at night, so theoretically no one should be on the property. Still, people might wander in, even though we had about a dozen *Private*

Property and *Keep Out* and *Video Surveillance* signs posted at every possible point of ingress.

I promised to keep my phone on me at all times.

Truthfully, I wasn't a guy who took a whole ton of risks. I wasn't going to go into the woods without someone with me. I wasn't going to take a canoe to paddle. I did swim, but only when the lake was calm. I liked my job and wasn't going to do anything to fuck with that—like dying in some stupid way. And plenty of people lived alone in these mountains, even though the hills north of Mission City were a bit of wilderness close to civilization.

Plus, I might be alone, but I certainly wasn't living rough. I had electricity, stellar internet, cable, and a gas fireplace should the power go out and I needed a source of heat.

Finn had dropped by to ensure I was aware of the campfire ban.

The super sexy firefighter had dropped a couple of broad hints along the way.

Okay, he'd come right out and said he was gay and might I be interested in drinks at the Brew Pub? If not as a date, then as friends.

That was yesterday. Had I not already made plans with Demetrius, I might've seriously considered the offer. Not as a date, of course, but another friend? I'd taken his personal number and put it in my phone. At the very least, as an out man in Mission City, he could give me a proper lay of the land.

Demetrius's minivan came into view, and my heart leapt.

Alessandra had texted twenty-three minutes ago to let me know Keegan and Alaina were settling in with Kyle and Paisley. My boss also sent a picture with Alaina holding Wesley and Keegan sitting next to his sister, clearly enamored with the toddler who apparently was not wanting to run around at that moment. He was evidently fascinated with the company. My boss had also wished me luck.

Luck?

She had no idea, of course. She just thought Demetrius was here as a potential suitor—her word, not mine. Telling my boss that I liked to dress up like a puppy and get belly scritches hadn't seemed like the best idea.

He exited his minivan, then opened the door to the back seat.

Be patient. He was never going to run into your arms and profess his undying love for you. And you wouldn't want him to.

Well, mostly.

He had given me back the books I'd bought for Wesley. I had yet to find a good time to give them to Alessandra. I wanted it to be a quiet moment where she might be honest about whether or not I'd made good choices. Dickens said he'd exchange them if I'd missed the mark.

Demetrius backed out of the minivan carrying...

A plant?

And a cooler bag.

He grinned.

I strode over to meet him.

"Oh great. You can take the plant."

I obeyed.

He continued to smile. "Are you okay if I grab my overnight bag?"

I nodded.

"Perfect." He opened the hatch, grabbed a gym bag, and shut the door. Then he locked the minivan "Probably not needed. That being said, did you see the video of the bear opening a car door? I mean, I don't keep food in there, but I still don't want a bear hunkering down in my baby."

"Uh..." I frowned. "I don't think I've seen that video."

"Oh? I think there are a couple. Alaina insisted on showing them to Keegan before he came to camp. Her way of ensuring he took food-storage safety seriously."

At that, I chuckled. "She sounds like quite the sister."

"She takes good care of us. Keegan's willing to let her lead a lot of the time. I wouldn't say he's a follower..."

"But he's happier when someone else makes the tough decisions." I opened the front door to my cabin and held it for Demetrius.

He stepped into the main room. "Well, sort of. He's *decided* he's not going back to his old school. He and Alaina have been at me pretty continuously about moving to Mission City."

Cody had mentioned Keegan's near-obsession about moving.

Knowing all about fresh starts, I couldn't blame the young man for wanting to make one. But he wasn't the only person in the family.

"I understand Alaina's best friend lives in Abbotsford?"

"Yep. Where should I put this?" He held up his gym bag.

I swallowed. "Bedroom is fine." He was the guest and would have the bedroom. Whether I stayed in there with him or slept on my pullout couch was a discussion for later.

"Cheers." He laid the cooler bag on the kitchen table and headed toward the bedroom.

I put the plant on the center of the table. "Uh, a plant?"

He was grinning when he returned from the bedroom. "Alessandra's recommendation. I thought flowers were classic, but they die. Allie, as she likes me to call her, suggested this." He gestured with a flourish.

"It kind of looks like a flower." All purple blooms and green leaves.

"It's an African Violet. Now, it's not a real violet, but we won't tell her that."

"Her?"

"Work with me."

"Right." I attempted a serious expression. "An African violet that isn't a violet. Got it."

He placed a pretty pamphlet on the table. *The Care and Feeding of Your African Violet*.

"Oh."

"In case you didn't know. I'll be honest—I loved Erlene, but she killed everything except her kids. After she passed, I never got around to adding plants. But I feel like you need some pretty in this place. Alessandra agreed."

Despite myself, I smiled. "You like the pretty?"

"I like you." Then he rolled his eyes. "Too cheesy. I wanted to bring buttercups, but the florist didn't sell them. In fact, she gave me a funny look when I asked."

Words escaped me. Of course he honored my pup name. He was Big D. Daddy D. *I never paid enough attention to him. I just assumed he'd always be there.* And I'd been in a committed relationship—as had he. Now wasn't the time for regrets. "African violets are perfect. I think there might be buttercups in the wild around here, but they mainly flower in the spring."

"We'll have to go hunting." He grinned.

Which implies you'll be around next spring, which is a hell of an assumption on your part and one that doesn't necessarily panic me.

"What would you like for dinner?" The family had hit the road early afternoon to escape the worst of the Friday traffic bailing out of Vancouver. At least it hadn't been a long weekend.

He grinned as he moved to the cooler bag. "I hope you didn't cook."

"I didn't." *I didn't want to seem presumptuous...like assuming you were staying when we hadn't even discussed that.*

"Great. Smith baked us a lasagna. Now, Alessandra said two things. One, that lasagna is a little heavy for a summer's evening—"

"I don't mind."

He chuckled. "Neither do I."

"And the other?"

"That she taste-tested it and, to her husband's credit, this was one of the best he's made. He made two trays, so they're having lasagna as well. Which is awesome because both Alaina and Keegan love the stuff." He pulled tinfoil-wrapped food from the cooler first. "Garlic bread."

"Yummy."

"Right? They didn't send salad but figured we could sort that out."

"I have fresh vegetables." Probably even the fixings for a green salad.

"So if you sort that, I'll put the lasagna in the oven to heat. Or should I put slices in the microwave? That way the place won't get too hot."

"Good thinking. I'll admit I microwave more than I cook."

"You must miss having Chef around."

I chuckled. "Having someone else do the cooking was lovely. The new campers will be here in just over a week."

"You must be so stoked." He grabbed two plates as I organized lettuce, tomatoes, green peppers, and carrots.

"I am. They look like a great group of kids. We've got a couple of trans teenagers, one enby, and seven others who identify as queer. I was worried about Makenna and Grey—since they're only a couple of years older than the oldest camper—but they've proven themselves. I mean, I want the campers to have fun. That said, I was grateful we didn't have any pranks with the last group."

"That's not really why the campers are here. At least I know hijinks wasn't on Keegan's list."

I rinsed the lettuce. "Cody gave me the same take. That might change from group to group—mostly depending on personalities. But this first group took their roles seriously."

"In what way?" Demetrius used a spatula to scoop the heavenly smelling lasagna onto plates.

"I guess...as the inaugural group, they wanted to set a good example. To enjoy their time, certainly, but to be good kids. To, I don't know...assure Smith and Alessandra that they did the right thing in opening the camp. Does that make sense?"

Slowly, he nodded. "That about fits with what Keegan said. He wanted to spend as much time as he could around people like himself. So he could learn what they were doing that worked. He also said your staff was amazing—which I'd already pretty much figured out."

I tore the lettuce into pieces. "The anonymous surveys from both parents and campers came back with encouraging words. A few really good suggestions as well. Stuff we can implement before the next camp."

"That's great." He put the first plate in the microwave. "Do you have two chopping blocks? I'm awesome with tomatoes."

"Fantastic, I'm good at peeling carrots." I handed him the tomato and a knife.

We washed our vegetables and then set about fixing them. He cut the tomatoes into chunks while, after I removed the top layer, I then peeled the carrot—planning to add the peels to the top of the salad. Since he finished first, he tackled the green pepper while I swapped out the lasagna and heated the garlic toast in my mini oven.

Within about fifteen minutes we had piping-hot lasagna, toasty garlic bread, and a fresh salad.

Demetrius assured me he was a fan of vinaigrette dressing, so all was perfect. He grinned after the first bite of lasagna. "Allie didn't lie."

I laughed. "No, she did not. If you text to check on the kids, maybe compliment Smith? This is amazing."

"It is. I still can't believe they offered to watch the kids for the night."

"I would've come into Vancouver if that was the only way to see you again."

He licked his lips. "I might've had to ask. The kids are okay for a few hours, but I don't want to leave them overnight." He held my gaze. "We've decided to move to Mission City."

My heart kicked into overdrive. "Oh?"

"Yeah. I would say it was two-against-one, but my heart wasn't in it. After two weeks in town, even though I was staying in the hotel, I could admit I saw us living here. It'll be an adjustment. For all of us. I've barely left Vancouver over the years. Born and raised. Then raised my sisters and now my kids. East Van is all I've ever known. And I haven't traveled much—not like you."

"Toronto and Nova Scotia are hardly traveling."

"You've never been anywhere but Canada?"

His question startled me. "Well, sure. Texas and New York for business. With the family to India every couple of years. Although my grandparents immigrated to Canada fifty years ago, my family still has strong ties to the old country. Obviously I haven't gone in about eight years. My last visit was the summer before my third year at university."

"Would you go back?"

I blinked. "As a tourist?"

"Well, yeah. Say if you had a couple of teenagers interested in getting outside of Vancouver...?"

"Uh, sure. I doubt I'd see my family. I mean, maybe my parents didn't tell them about me...but I haven't done anything to keep in contact with them. I sort of assumed everything had been severed."

"If going back would be too painful—"

"It's not that." I shook my head. "Until I took this job, I didn't have the resources to pay for a trip. To visit a country I've been to almost a dozen times and family members who might reject me." I looked away. To the sliding glass doors at the back of the cabin that led to a little private outdoor space that was away from the campers and prying eyes. "We should've eaten outside."

"And get eaten ourselves by bugs?"

"I have stuff for that." I directed my gaze back to him. "If you want to take Keegan and Alaina to India, I think that's a great idea."

"I'm getting ahead of myself." He laid his fork by his plate. "I'm trying to discover more about you."

"Just ask, Demetrius. Despite the fact I hold myself apart—for reasons we both know—I'm actually pretty honest about my life."

"Okay." He picked up his fork and poked at the last bite of lasagna. "Did you ever play again? After your last visit to What'sUp Pup?"

I speared a piece of lettuce with my fork. "That's a loaded question. The simple—and obvious—answer is no. Gary threw away all my equipment, costumes, and toys. Everything was gone when I packed up my things. Well, I assume he threw them out." I eyed the lettuce. "I went to the Mission City Library and finally did an incognito internet search for him. Turns out he's in jail for embezzlement. Millions of dollars. I was like..." I flailed my arm around. "I've only been gone six years. Fraud usually takes a long time to discover and investigate. Unless the fraudster is stupid and gets caught easily."

"Well, you probably have your answer." He swirled some cheese onto his fork. "So, no regrets?" He offered me a devious smile.

"I did the search before we went to Stavros's. I thought he might've been the one to leave the dog treats—that he somehow knew I was back and was taunting me."

Demetrius's fork clattered to the plate. "Jesus. I never thought...I was just..." He rubbed his face. "I'm so fucking sorry."

"You had no way of knowing. I got the gifts, and I panicked. If not Gary—"

"The Gnat."

"—the Gnat." Somehow, that made me smile. "Yeah, him. But if not him, then who?"

"I thought you recognized me but weren't saying anything. I just...wanted to give you something. To remind you of our time together. To remind you of happy moments."

"Yeah." I sipped my water. "So that was unexpected for me. And buying treats for Queenie and Taffy was the first time I'd stepped into a pet store in six years. That...hurt. I love being Buttercup. I just don't know if he can be part of me anymore."

Demetrius also sipped his water. "Well, we've got twenty-four hours to figure that out—if you're game."

Intrigued, I cocked my head.

He smiled. "Okay, I didn't bring my overnight bag into your cabin because I didn't want to be presumptuous. I'll do that after I show you what's in my bag—if you want me to stay. Otherwise, nabbing a room at The Grand won't be a hardship. Or you can throw me in a cabin here for the night—I promise to behave."

"You're thinking I'm going to kick you out?"

He shrugged. "I'm never quite sure what's going to happen in life. I can plan and try to predict and do my best to influence things. In the end, though, I feel like I have little control. I mean, I can make the proactive decision to move to Mission City—after my kids spend four days hounding me. I can make appointments to see five houses tomorrow morning with a realtor and then take the kids to see the top couple of contenders, but I can't guarantee our perfect house is out there."

Again, my heart rate increased. He was serious. He was moving to Mission City.

"You're selling your place in Vancouver?"

He shook his head. Then nodded. "When I talked to Alessandra about this insanity—because she's a really easy person to talk to—"

"It's the social worker in her."

"There is that. Anyway, she recommended that realtor, Cadence Crawford, to help me find a place in Mission City and he, in turn, knew a realtor named Juanita in Vancouver. She normally handles, uh, expensive places. But as favor to Cadence, she's taking my sale. She's in there with a staging crew today. I told her to leave the kids' rooms as they were, but to do whatever needed to be done with the rest of the place."

"You're not letting grass grow under your feet."

"Nope." He popped the *p*. "I've got schools to register the kids in. Extracurricular activities to sign up for."

"Your work...?" I still wasn't entirely certain what he did.

"Work from home on a flexible schedule. As long as I'm in Canada, I'm good."

I wasn't going to ask. If he wanted to share, he would. "So that's that?" Things felt like they were moving at lightning speed.

"Only to do with me and the kids. They made their case. I listened. I explained the reality of their choice. They pretended to listen. We came to an agreement. But that doesn't affect you and me." He gestured between us both. "Whether we even see each other again is entirely up to you."

"But you want to see me?" *He's here, right? So that's a pretty stupid question.*

"I do. I want to feel out what kind of relationship we might have. I'm as attracted to you as I was six years ago. Only now I'm free to take it beyond Daddy/pup play in a club. But you need to tell me what you want. Because frankly, Jai, I don't see you as an open book. I see a man who's been hurt. A man in need of love and healing. Whether that involves puppy play, some kind of physical intimacy, both, or neither will be entirely up to you. I can be your friend, your lover, your Daddy. Just one of those or all three. Or some combination. I know it'll be incredibly challenging—you've got camp and I've got the kids. They know nothing about my lifestyle. I've told them I'm bisexual—so that part of any relationship won't come as a surprise. That's if you even want them to know. But I'll warn you now, I don't like secrets."

"I don't like secrets either."

He nodded. "So we're in agreement."

Having that out of the way, my impish nature burst through. "Is Big D going to show me what's in his bag?"

An eyebrow shot up, followed by a huge grin. "Pup, I thought you'd never ask."

Chapter Twenty

Demetrius

I ordered my cock to *stand down* as I cleaned the dishes and put away the leftovers.

At my insistence, Jai was in the bedroom *preparing* himself.

Although I found it challenging for me to be hands off, I left the interpretation of that verb to him.

"I'm ready, Big D." His voice came in sharp, excited yips.

I dried my hands on a tea towel, after having washed them, and sauntered into the bedroom. I'd removed my shoes earlier, but was still fully dressed. I didn't know where tonight was going to lead—

Apparently to some interesting places.

Jai was on all fours on the bed.

Naked.

He'd pulled back the comforter, so he was just on the top sheet. And apparently he'd dug through my bag, because all the contents were laid out before him on the mattress.

I put my hands on my hips. "You know, I had plans."

He grinned up at me mischievously. "Puppy likes to explore."

"Puppy likes to get into trouble." He'd always been a scamp.

He shrugged. "That's why you brought me home." His dark-brown eyes shone.

From this angle, I couldn't see *all* of him, but I didn't mind. We had all the time in the world.

Or, well, about fifteen hours.

Realtor waiting to see me in the morning and all that.

I grasped the first object. "Does pup want a collar?"

He nodded.

"This is just a training collar." Because I didn't want him to think that me putting this around his neck meant he was committing to something more serious.

"I know." He batted his eyes. "I want Daddy to train me."

His words stilled me. Before, he'd called me *Big D*. To make the switch meant something...or at least it did to me.

I cocked my head.

He held my gaze.

Okay. He's well aware of what he's saying and what the ramifications are.

I placed the yellow sparkly collar around his neck and secured it. "My beautiful Buttercup."

He ducked his head in evident shyness. At times, in the past, he'd been brash and playful. Other times, he'd been reflective and soulful. Him having to shove those memories away after Gary—shoving me away—hurt my heart. I wanted to give him everything.

This was our second chance.

I grasped the paws.

He extended his hands to let me put them on. As I did, his grin increased.

Seeing him incandescent with happiness lit something within me. So I grasped the floppy ears.

He ducked his head so I could attach them. His nose twitched. "Woof!"

"Yes, pup, you look beautiful." I sat on the edge of the bed. I fingered the bag of treats. "These are still your favorites?"

Enthusiastic nodding that nearly dislodged the ears.

I chuckled as I righted them. "And I remember you had a preference for squeaky toys over balls—although sometimes I could convince you to play with both."

He blinked several times.

"I remember, Buttercup. I remember everything about you. I treasured every moment I had with you." I missed the simplicity of our time at the club. I knew how to make pups feel good and safe. I didn't feel nearly as confident in dealing with the complexity of teenagers. In essence, I'd suppressed my Daddy tendencies when I'd become a real father. Pups had taken a back seat to skinned knees, rollerblades, and grieving over losing Erlene.

Now, I had a chance to recapture what I was missing.

I snagged a squeaky toy and squeezed.

His eyes lit.

"Why don't you play for a bit?"

More enthusiastic head bobbing.

I held the toy out.

He snagged it between his teeth.

"Would you mind if I sit on the bed and watch you play?"

He shook his head.

I propped a pillow against the headboard, sat, and stretched my long legs out before me.

After a moment, he squeezed his toy between his teeth.

It squeaked.

He vibrated with excitement. Then he continued chomping on it and shaking his head as if to dislodge it.

Slowly, I petted his hair.

His luminous eyes stared up at me.

"Do you want scritches? You were playing, and I don't want to interrupt, but I thought you might want cuddles—"

He launched himself into my lap.

I *oofed* as he landed on me. Then he laid his head against my chest.

Without needing any further encouragement, I ran my hand through his hair, using my nails on his scalp. Then I scratched up and down his back, reveling in the soft skin. Of all the pups, he'd always had the softest skin. Almost delicate to the touch—yet he loved the rough and tumble as much as the quiet moments of bonding and connection.

I blinked back tears. I had Buttercup in my lap. My boy was back where he belonged. Only this time we didn't have artificial barriers. We had never exchanged real names at the club. I was Daddy D and he was Buttercup. We didn't know each other beyond that. Now? Jai knew about my kids. I had a better understanding of why he'd had to stop coming to the club. He'd moved away. Erlene died.

Yet we'd found our way back to each other.

But, we were different people.

He sniffed.

"Are you okay?" I cupped his cheek.

"Woof."

I smiled. "I don't know what that means. I'll take it as happiness."

"It is." He smiled, then ducked his head a little shyly. "Might you..." He bit his lower lip.

"Might I...?"

"Might you get undressed?"

I stilled. I'd only planned for play, because that was all we'd ever done. Plenty of Daddies and pups brought sex into the relationship. I'd never crossed that line with anyone. Partly because I was committed to Erlene, for certain, but mostly because no one had ever made me want to make the leap.

He gazed up at me through those impossibly long lashes. "Daddy was very generous with me the other night. I want to return the favor."

The night of the blow job. Apparently that medical crisis had been the most excitement at camp all week, and things had run smoothly the rest of the time—which I appreciated. Jai didn't need more drama in his life.

"You want Daddy to...?"

"I want Daddy's cock in my mouth. If that's okay." He added that quickly.

We'd never played in any sexual manner before—although plenty of people did. I'd witnessed many a pup being debauched. I'd never considered doing that with Jai.

That's kind of not true. But you kept your distance because you'd heard he wasn't looking for that. You were being respectful. Now he's asking for more. Neither of us had any reason to ignore what was happening between the two of us. My kids were safe. He didn't have any obligations.

"Daddy can undress." For just a moment, Jai's expression turned serious—with his brow furrowing. "I, uh, have supplies. Not that I'm obligating you...just letting you know what the options are. Oh, and before you undress—" He held my gaze. "Maybe you want to bring your *other* bag in? I'm asking you to stay the night." The *if you want* remained unspoken, but hung in the air.

"You're certain?" We'd hardly spent any time in each other's company during the past three weeks. I didn't want to make assumptions.

"I'm sure." He squeaked his toy. "I'm really sure." Then he flopped like a starfish onto his belly, grabbed the squeaky bone in his mouth, and started chomping.

Naturally, I'd been very careful about buying expensive nontoxic toys.

I rose from the bed, made my way out to the vehicle, retrieved my overnight bag containing toiletries and clothes for tomorrow, and then returned to the cabin. After carefully locking the door and ensuring all the windows were covered, I headed to the bedroom.

To find Buttercup chomping on his toy.

"You're going to dislodge the squeaker." I'd bought one of the strongest I could. And dogs' teeth were pretty sharp, but clearly he was on a mission.

He stopped, grinned, and resumed his task.

Smiling, I slowly unbuttoned my shirt. I'd gone a little dressier than he'd seen me before. I snagged a hanger from the closet and secured the shirt. Then I emptied my pockets. I'd charged my phone in the minivan on the way from Vancouver, so I had a full charge.

I glanced at the screen.

—*Kids are great. All is well. Enjoy and we'll talk tomorrow morning.*
—

From Alessandra. Of course. Because she understood in a way I was only beginning to.

Jai could be my one.

I sent back a thumbs-up emoji—because what could I say? *Thank you for giving me this time? Thank you for caring for the most important people in my life? Thank you for giving me clarity when I needed that most? Finally, thank you for your friendship.* I was quite certain befriending parents wasn't on her to-do list. Yet she'd done it.

After removing my khakis, I hung them in the closet as well. Off came my socks, and I stood there in just my boxer briefs.

"Woof." A little lasciviously.

I smiled, hooked my boxers with my thumbs, and dragged them down.

Mindful of my growing erection.

Truthfully, I hadn't counted on anything sexual tonight. My goal had been to get Jai comfortable with his Buttercup again. If that was all we got to tonight, I'd still be the happiest man on the planet.

Jai pulled his arms and then his legs into his torso and, in one graceful movement, was back on all fours. "Yum."

My cock filled completely.

I moved toward the side of the bed.

He advanced toward me. He met, and held, my gaze.

I nodded.

He grinned, licked his lips, and positioned himself so his lips were a mere inch away from my cock.

I leaned forward to close the distance.

He grasped the base of my shaft, then licked the tip.

Pleasure raced through me. My mind tried to compute the last time this had happened—with a man or a woman—and it drew a blank. Years. So many years.

He swirled his tongue around my crown.

I bucked.

His eyes flashed triumph as he took me into his mouth.

With his enthusiasm, I didn't need to ask if he was okay with this. I didn't need to wonder if the power dynamic was off. Because, despite all evidence to the contrary, he was absolutely the one in control of this encounter. Either of us could call it off, obviously. Neither of us was going to, apparently.

He sucked me deeper, continuing to work me with his tongue. At one point, he speared my slit, and I bucked again.

I placed a hand on his head—both to steady myself, but also to offer gentle encouragement. Oh, and to feel his silky strands under my fingers. A memory invaded—of holding him close and petting him when he'd clearly had a bad day. I'd wondered, of course, but hadn't asked. Generally, he'd chosen to be nonverbal when he'd played. Plenty of yips, barks, and other doggie sounds—but never actual words. Would he have spilled about his life? I just didn't have an answer to that question.

He raked his teeth along my length.

I moaned.

His sucking continued with abandon as he continued to bring me all the pleasure.

I had plans for him to come later—if I could stay awake. I tended to fall asleep after sex. Especially if I was stressed. Pretty much every moment since Keegan had first been bullied had been anxiety-provoking for me. And since we'd all arrived home Monday, and the kids had started the *convince Dad to move to Mission City* campaign? A lot of thinking and, if I was honest, a lot of stress.

He hummed—clearly enjoying himself—and that was enough to tip me over the edge.

"I'm coming, Buttercup. Pull off if—"

He redoubled his efforts, hollowing his cheeks and sucking harder.

Taking that as permission, I let myself go. My balls drew up and, within moments, I was coming in his mouth.

He swallowed as I emptied.

Yet a feeling of fullness overwhelmed me. Fullness in my heart. Fullness in my soul. Fullness of all the future possibilities.

After pulling off me with a pop, Jai swept all the toys, treats, and leash off the end of the bed where they clattered to the floor. He sat back on his haunches and offered his hand.

I took it.

He guided me to the bed.

I lay down.

He pulled the comforter over us and curled into my side.

"What about—"

After pressing a paw covered finger to my mouth to silence me, he pressed his lips to mine. Finally, he pulled back. "Rest now, talk later."

We were barely at seven o'clock, but my eyelids were heavy.

"Yes, that."

He grinned and laid his head against my shoulder.

Within moments, I was out.

Chapter Twenty-One

Jai

Daddy didn't snore. Which, frankly, surprised me. He was such a big guy—although broad and tall—not fat. Curling against him made me warm inside and out.

I've missed you. Yes, I should have recognized you. I think my heart did, but my mind wouldn't go there. Six years is a long time. You always wore a mask...but mostly I didn't want to believe you were back in my life and I couldn't have you.

Doing the right thing was always my stance. Being able to hold my head high, even when everything around me was falling apart. Staying apart from Demetrius for the past three weeks had been brutal.

Okay, except the brief interlude in the Grand Hotel.

When he'd calmed me by ordering me with doggie commands, I'd suddenly known. Not only who he was, but that my instincts had been spot-on—he was someone I could be with.

I want to grab that special toy.

My mind continued to obsess about it. The one I focused on hadn't been purchased at a pet store. Nope. Either a fetish store in Vancouver or over the internet.

After more contemplation, I slid from his grasp.

He murmured, but didn't wake.

Man, he really sleeps after sex. Have to remember that. Frankly, I was a little flattered. That I'd wiped him out so thoroughly.

I knelt on the floor and lovingly collected everything. I was certain he'd understood I wasn't dismissing them when I'd summarily removed them. I wanted to be ready for anything. A blow job and cuddling would've been challenging with all the wonderful things he'd brought for me. He'd understood I had none of my old gear—and he'd been right.

After snagging the most precious of all the gifts, I grasped the bottle of lube from my nightstand, and I crept into the bathroom. I removed my paws and my ears, then pissed, flushed the toilet, and then ran the water hot as I washed my hands. The butt plug with the tail attached still in the wrapper, but I still ran it through the hot water for a bit.

Satisfied I'd basically sterilized it, I grabbed the lube.

The rest was just muscle memory—preparing myself, preparing the plug, inserting the—

Yep.

My previously neglected prostate was super happy.

I'd been ignoring him for about six years and he was now expressing his displeasure at that omission. I'd jerked off occasionally, but I hadn't gone near the rest of me. Sometimes memories were just overwhelming, so I continuously shoved them away where they couldn't hurt me.

Or so you told yourself.

Yeah, I was good at lying to myself. Deluding myself. Telling myself things that weren't true. Like that I'd deserved what had happened to me. Like I was a bad person. Like no one would ever love me. Just as Jai. Let alone the man who liked to dress up like a pup and seek affection that way.

"Are you okay?"

I startled at Demetrius's question. He was out of sight, clearly giving me space, but also concerned.

"Just a second." I washed my hands thoroughly, then grabbed the bottle of lube. I glanced into the mirror. My cheeks were a little ruddy. My eyes were a little bright. But no tears. No recriminations or second thoughts. Nope, I'd made my decision, and I was okay with that. I opened the door.

He stood, naked, on the other side of the door. He was leaning against the doorjamb and waited patiently. "I didn't want to interrupt...but you were gone a long time. I was hoping..." He took a deep breath.

I stepped into his space, wrapped my arms around his waist, and laid my head on his chest—over his heart.

Without a moment's hesitation, he wrapped me in a bear hug. "Oh, Buttercup."

"Will you take me to bed?"

He pulled back and gazed into my eyes. He feathered my already messy hair, then patted my rump above my tail. "I won't ask you if you're sure, because I've figured out what you were up to. Clever boy." He pressed a kiss to my nose. "Let me do what I need to do and then I'll join you."

Inside, I did a little happy dance. Inserting the tail had been a risk. Well, so had been greeting him naked when he'd first stepped into the bedroom. Apparently both had been risks worth taking. "I'll be waiting, Daddy." I pressed a kiss to his cheek, enjoying the stubble—dark with the odd white whisker. I'd shaved before he arrived, so I was still smooth. The contrast reminded me of the age difference, the Daddy difference.

I headed to the bedroom. In the end, I chose to face the headboard with my butt sticking in the air. My cock stiffened and my balls became heavy as I thought of all the things he was going to—

Condoms. Shit. I snagged a couple and dropped them onto the mattress beside me. I'd been tested several times since Gary the Gnat had turfed me.

God, I loved Daddy's name for my jackass ex.

I'd also had a thorough physical before taking this job. All negative and completely healthy.

Assuming Daddy was too was a risk I wasn't willing to take. Did I hope to one day go bareback? Certainly. Just not today. *How long has it been for him? Has he had lovers since Erlene? Men? Women?* None of my business, per se, but I wanted to know what he'd been through. I wanted to be someone he could talk to.

"Oh, that's the most beautiful sight." His entrance had been silent.

Now, though, I felt a shift in the energy in the room. I wiggled my butt, feeling the tail swish against my thighs.

"Buttercup, you have the most glorious ass." He grasped my cheeks in both hands.

I envisioned him—with his dark hands against my tanned skin. The stunning contrast we made. We'd lived such very different lives—and yet we'd somehow found each other. I still couldn't fathom that.

He grasped the base of the plug and slowly rotated it.

My cock leaked a drop of precum onto the sheet.

"Pup likes that?"

"Oh yes, Daddy. I need you to make me yours. I need to belong to you." *For now and forever.* Because I saw us together. I didn't know if that meant I'd have a place in Keegan's and Alaina's life. I certainly hoped I would, but that would be up to Demetrius.

He slowly withdrew the plug almost all the way out, then gently slid it back in.

My prostate sang in pleasure. Heat raced to my cheeks and sparks exploded in my spine. "Please, Daddy...make me feel good."

"Oh, Buttercup. You have no idea how happy that request makes me. Daddy will always take care of you."

Did he realize what he'd said? Always *was a big word. I'm ready...but is he?*

Slowly, rotating gently, he removed the plug.

A feeling of bereavement overwhelmed me. *Be patient. He won't make you wait long.*

And he didn't. As I glanced over my shoulder, he tore open the wrapper and rolled the condom on.

I faced front again.

The mattress dipped as he settled himself behind me. He squeezed my ass cheeks again, the nudged my hole with his cockhead.

"I can't express how beautiful you are—inside and out." He pressed into me. "And I'm so proud of you. You're the best pup in the world."

I'm not. I'm a flawed pup. A broken person. I don't know if I can be the person you need me to be.

"Bear down, Buttercup. And remember to breathe."

Because it hurt. It really hurt. Six years was a damn long time and although the plug had helped, it wasn't nearly as big as Daddy. I'd noted his size and girth when I'd given him the blow job. Had imagined how he'd feel inside me.

And now I knew.

"Just a little bit now."

His crown finished breaching me, and I let out a sigh of relief.

Again, in infinitesimal increments, he pressed into me. Then he'd pull back a bit. Then push farther. Each pass of his shaft over my prostate filled me with a pleasure I'd long forgotten.

He murmured, "I'm home."

Yes, he was.

Truly.

"I'm ready, Daddy."

"Good pup." He grasped my hips and began thrusting and withdrawing. Over and over. He was chasing the same orgasm I was. Then he reached around to snag my cock. He jerked me to the same unrelenting rhythm he set. His breathing hitched. "Buttercup, I need you to come."

Since I did as well, I let myself go. My balls drew up, and I spurted all over Daddy's hand.

He thrust one last time and held himself still as he came inside me.

I fought to catch my breath.

He shuddered. "I, uh..."

"Yeah."

Slowly, and with great care—as he did everything—he withdrew. He lay on the bed next to me and pulled me toward him.

I grabbed the comforter first, as the fan was moving the chilly night air, and cocooned us under it.

He spooned me.

I sighed.

"You're..." He feathered his hand through my damp hair and then pressed a kiss to my shoulder. "Damn, condom." He shifted away and then, after a moment, returned. He pulled me even closer. "Do you think you can sleep?"

"Do you always fall asleep immediately after sex?"

"Uh..." A yawn. "Maybe. It doesn't have anything to do with you."

"Oh, really? I'm insulted. I'd like to think I wrung an orgasm from you that sapped all your energy and made you pass out." I added a teasing tone to my voice.

"That you did." Said on a yawn.

I pressed my hand to his thigh. "Sleep now, Daddy. We can talk in the morning."

"Okay." Yet another yawn.

I smiled to myself as I tried to subtly adjust away from the wet spot. We really should be showering and changing the sheets, but his firm grasp on me allowed me to slip into sleep as well.

Chapter Twenty-Two

Demetrius

"Yes, I'm certain I want you to come with me." I scraped the bit of crust I hadn't eaten into Jai's compost container. "I'm meeting Cadence Crawford at the first house in forty minutes. Enough time to grab a Starbucks coffee."

He arched an eyebrow. "You've had two cups already."

I shrugged. "I want a caramel macchiato."

"Ah."

"And we can get you a black coffee at Starbucks or Timmie's. But only if we head out now."

He eyed me dubiously.

"I mean, unless you have something else to do. I'm being kind of presumptuous—just assuming you can drop everything and come with me."

"First, it's Saturday, and I don't have any campers. Even I get a day off."

"Okay." I waited.

"Secondly, of course I want to come with you. But this is a family thing."

"Right. We'll narrow it down to two or three and then talk to the kids. The thing is...I don't know Mission City."

"Cadence does. I realized I went to school with him."

"Yeah?"

He put the last dish in the dishwasher. "I went to school with a lot of people. Some of whom moved away and never came back. Some of whom never left."

"And some who moved away and *then* came back."

"Yeah." He met my gaze. "The town has changed. Remember, I went away ten years ago. First for university and then for...other stuff. I didn't come home much."

On impulse, I held open my arms.

He didn't disappoint. He stepped right into them and rested his head above my heart. "Things will have changed."

"And Cadence can take us through that. Some things won't have changed—like I don't want your parents as neighbors." I chuckled. "But I mentioned Arnav and Foster's neighborhood. It's at the top of my price range, but it's doable."

"That's a great neighborhood—and near Cedar Street Elementary school. A bit of a longer walk to the high school, but not much."

"Cadence said all that. There are two houses in that area we're looking at. I can certainly drive the kids to school, but I'm trying to give them more independence."

"Because you're a good dad." He pulled back and met my gaze. "If you're sure."

"I am." No matter the role he might play in my life, I wanted his input. I trusted him. "So do you want to drive or should I?"

"If you drive, I can review the houses you're looking at."

"Great." I pulled my keys out of my pocket. "Are you okay with me leaving the toys and gifts? They're for you, after all." I wanted him to feel comfortable. I knew having his toys had ended in betrayal before.

"I have a safe."

"I'm glad to hear that." I grinned. "Why don't you put them away while I pack up my things and then we can get on the road? Timmie's or Starbucks or both?"

"I suppose I could try a caramel macchiato." He arched an eyebrow.

"You'll love it." I pressed a kiss to his cheek.

Ten minutes later we were on the road.

Twenty minutes after that, we got our coffees.

Five minutes after that glorious task was accomplished, we met with Cadence.

Three hours later, we'd seen four houses.

The suggested fifth had been six blocks from Jai's parents. Different neighborhoods—and different median income levels—but Keegan would have to walk within a block of their house.

Hard no.

In the end, the two from Arnav and Foster's area were the best choices. Hell, one was on their street.

We stood on the street before the available house closest to my new friends.

Cadence texted furiously while Jai and I sipped our waters.

"Alessandra and Smith want to meet us for lunch at Fifties. If that's okay." I checked my phone. "Well, late lunch. She said the kids have had a light snack. Paisley and Kyle are going to stay behind to watch a soccer match. Apparently they're obsessed and want to watch the game live."

Jai pursed his lips. "Again, are you sure you want me there? I can grab a cab home—"

I snagged his hand with my one that wasn't clutching my phone. "I know we haven't talked. But I want you in my life. It'll be up to you in what capacity—"

"Okay!" Cadence strode over. "I managed to finagle us appointments at three and four o'clock."

"Uh, that was generous of them." I didn't know much about real estate, but leaving one's house twice in a day was a pain.

"I was honest and said we were down to two and likely to put in an offer shortly." He met my gaze. "Your mortgage person at the credit union has everything organized, right?"

"Yep."

"And I can draw up the offer as soon as you make a decision. We'll make it contingent on financing and a home inspection. Both the houses are newer, but I want you to have a clear picture of what you're dealing with."

"I've contacted the inspection company, and they can send someone on Monday."

"Perfect. So we're good." He clapped his hands.

"Do you want to come to lunch as well? Meet the kids?"

He grinned. "I never turn down an offer to meet new people. I heard you say Alessandra?"

"Yep."

"Alessandra and Smith MacLean?"

"Yep. "

"I helped them find their home."

I laughed. "Oh, wow. That must have been an interesting search."

"Not really. I found out the house was about to go onto the market, and it had everything they were looking for—and anything else that might come up, they could, frankly afford to do themselves. So Smith offered over the asking price, and the house never officially went on the market. We'd been scouting empty lots, but in the end, he wanted something quick."

I considered commenting Cadence probably did very well on that transaction—the house was massive and on a huge plot of land—but that might be crass. "They were lucky to have you."

"They're good people. Alessandra's from Mission City and did some great work with social services. Now she does different stuff, but it's always to help people. I think Pride Camp is a fantastic idea. I wish it had been around when I was growing up. Okay." He clapped his hands. "Lunch?"

"Fifties."

His eyes lit. "Oh wow. My fave. I'll meet you down there. I just have to make a quick phone call."

"Great." I pocketed my phone, belatedly realizing I still held Jai's hand.

Our gazes met as Cadence walked away.

"Come with me?"

"Sure." He offered a shy smile.

Thirty minutes later, five adults and two kids crowded into a booth. Wesley, in his high chair, had the most space.

I couldn't have been happier.

After we'd placed our order with Sarabeth, Cadence produced the specs for both houses and passed them to Alaina and Keegan.

Both scrutinized each one. They sat between Jai, who was against the wall, and Alessandra who was on the end busily feeding her son some applesauce.

I sat between Smith and Cadence on the other side.

"Houses?" Keegan pointed to the pictures. "With actual backyards and grass and—"

"Duh." Alaina rolled her eyes.

I cleared my throat.

"Sorry." She pushed her sheet back. "And we're going to see them after lunch?"

I nodded. "Now, I don't want you to pay attention to the paint color and furniture, okay? We can repaint anything, and you'll be bringing your own things." Or I'd be buying new stuff for them—if I could fit it into the budget.

"And it's three blocks from my new school?" Alaina eyed me "French Immersion, right? Mom said French was so important. She fought to get us into the program." Spots were limited in Vancouver, and twice Erlene had engaged in what was essentially the hunger games to get her kids into the school.

She'd succeeded. And been so proud of herself.

You did so right by them, sweet lady. I hope I can do the same. "Yes. I've already put your name on the list. Regardless of where we live, you'll be going to this school. I just might have to drive you, or you might have to take the bus."

Alaina wrinkled her nose. "I don't want to do either of those things."

"No, I know that. That's why Cadence focused on this neighborhood. There are other houses. We're not in a rush."

"Unless that nice lady sells our condo." Alaina held my gaze.

"And I'm eight blocks away from my school?" Keegan continued to stare at the paper before him. "Uphill on the way home?"

"I can come and get you, or you can take the bus."

"I can walk it." He tipped his chin up.

"I know you can." My little boy wasn't so little anymore. And Alaina was growing like a weed. New clothes for everyone next month before they started school.

"My new friends Arnav and Foster live nearby. They have a dog."

"Can we have a dog?" Alaina's eyes widened. "We weren't even allowed a cat in the condo. Oh, can we get a dog?"

Jai's gaze shot to mine.

I smiled slowly, then refocused on the kids. "That's entirely possible. A rescue, though, okay?"

"I know a great trainer I can put you in touch with." Cadence grinned. "Torah Dixon."

Jai rolled his eyes. "Older sister to Sunshine."

The woman who worked at The Owl's Nest. See? I was getting it. "Let's rescue the dog first. There are several animal-control offices across the Vancouver area and into Cedar Valley. Obviously we want a dog who is good with kids."

Alaina put her hands on her hips. "We're not kids."

Jai blinked.

I smiled. "Sorry. Young adults."

Alessandra chuckled. "They grow up so fast."

Wesley chortled.

Cadence and Smith laughed.

I held Jai's gaze. *Break the news to the kids now or in private?* Alaina'd been quite taken with my...friend? Boyfriend? Lover?

Keegan kept casting his gaze between the two of us.

Yeah, he knew.

"So..."

"Okay, I've got everyone's food. Going to take a couple of trips." Sarabeth spent the next few minutes getting everyone settled.

When everyone was happily munching, I ventured, "How would you feel if Jai spent time with us?"

Alaina rolled her eyes. "It's so obvious you're a couple. Like, finally." She continued eating her fries.

Keegan blinked.

Shit.

"Mom wanted you to find someone else after she died." He sighed. "You knew that?"

"She asked me to make sure you did. Like I was a little matchmaker or something." He rolled his eyes. Then he smiled. "She was a romantic."

Love bloomed in my chest. "Yeah, she was."

Smith subtly pressed his shoulder to mine.

I blinked.

Jai smiled shyly.

Alessandra winked.

Yeah. We're going to be okay.

Chapter Twenty-Three

Jai

I would never have suggested Demetrius drop that little bombshell in a crowded restaurant in front of strangers. His kids needed time to process. To express how they really felt.

Or so I'd believed.

Then Keegan said his mother had asked him to make sure his father found someone new to love. As far as he was concerned, apparently, he was off the hook.

Erlene never should have put that on his shoulders.

But if the end result was casual acceptance, I might be coming around.

Now we stood in front of D's favorite of the two top choices. Alessandra, Smith, and Wesley had headed home after lunch.

We'd loaded the kids' bags into their dad's trunk and driven here—Alaina chatting the entire way, sharing everything she had learned about Mission City.

I'd caught Keegan's gaze in the rearview mirror, expecting exasperation. Instead, he had a grin on his face. Something I had seen at camp—something I was grateful to see now.

"The other house was nice." Alaina scrutinized the front of the second house we'd seen. "But I prefer this one. I love the front porch. We can sit out here with the dog—"

"On a leash." Keegan's contribution. He was very safety conscious. Almost too much. Something probably stemming from his mother's untimely death. Something we'd have to keep an eye on.

"Right." Alaina rolled her eyes. "But we can sit out here." She gestured up and down the street. Several clusters of kids were doing...kid stuff. She turned to her dad. "Where do your new friends live?"

He pointed three houses over and across the street. "Arnav is best friends with Jai."

She pivoted her attention to me. "Your friend who owns the dog?"

"Yes."

"Can we go meet the dog?"

"We can go knock. Cadence and your dad have adult stuff to talk about."

Demetrius met my gaze. "You like?"

"It's your decision."

He arched an eyebrow.

"Front porches are lovely for sitting and watching the world go by. A couple of rocking chairs and you're good."

Cadence chuckled.

"Yeah, you're right." Demetrius squeezed Alaina's shoulder. "Good call." He pivoted his attention to Keegan.

"As long as I get the blue room. I don't want to repaint it—I love that color."

That bedroom happened to be a bit larger than the one Alaina would likely choose. The fourth would be for Demetrius's office.

"I like the yellow room. Can I keep that color?" Alaina turned to me. "I don't do pink."

Cadence smothered a laugh.

I offered a bright smile. "Neither do I. I'm all about yellow or green."

"Well then that big bedroom is perfect for you and Dad." She pointed. "You said, dog?"

I blinked. *Just like that? You and my dad are going to share a room? There's no way that's normal. Kids don't just accept huge changes like that.*

Demetrius caught my gaze as if asking what I thought.

I tried to convey my panic.

"Alaina?" He watched her as she turned to him. "You're okay with Jai...?"

She rolled her eyes. "It's so obvious. And, like, I want you to be happy. He obviously makes you happy."

It couldn't possibly be that simple.

Keegan held up his hand. "Like, I'm supposed to say it's weird, right? My camp director moving in. Except Allie said we'd have a lot of changes. And that maybe making them all at once wasn't a bad thing. If we're pushing too hard..." He tapped his sister's shoulder.

"It's not that." Demetrius gazed back and forth between his kids. "We shouldn't have sprung this on you."

"Is there ever a good time?" He held his dad's gaze. "You taught me to accept who I was. I figure that goes for us accepting who you are."

I held my breath.

Alaina scrunched her nose. "So you said two dogs." As if she was quite over the *move in with my dad* conversation and ready to move on with what was really important.

"Queenie. She, uh, loves kids. Taffy lives next door. She might come over." Because if they weren't going to make a big deal out of it, I wouldn't either. I had to trust Alessandra had known what she was doing.

Keegan's eyes widened. "Two dogs? That's so cool."

I said a silent apology to Arnav and Foster for potentially disrupting them, but led the kids across the street.

Then that big bedroom is perfect for you and Dad. Just this easy acceptance from a young woman that she'd be sharing her father with a strange man. Keegan at least knew me—I was a complete outsider to Alaina. I couldn't get over this.

We rang the bell and a chorus of barks came from inside the house. "I'd say it's safe to assume Taffy's over. Or another dog."

"Oh hush." A voice came from behind the door.

Foster's?

"I've got them." A female voice.

"Thanks Stephanie."

Yep, Foster.

The front door opened and he greeted us with a grin. "What a lovely surprise!"

"You don't mind—"

"Not at all. But I recommend you come inside before our wonderful pooches try to make a run for it." He grinned as he beckoned us in and shut the door. "On their own, Queenie or Taffy would never bolt. Together? They're hellbent on escaping."

A stunning blonde woman loosened her grip on the dogs' collars once the door shut.

Queenie attempted to make a beeline for Alaina, who had already dropped to her knees, and Taffy eyed Keegan.

"We should be making proper introductions." The woman crouched. "Queenie, this is..."

"Alaina." The girl held her hands in her lap, but clearly wanted the dog's attention.

"Right. Queenie, friend."

The dog's tongue lolled. She gazed up at Foster.

He nodded.

She sniffed Alaina's hand. Then rubbed against it.

"You can pet her." Foster smiled.

"Thanks." Alaina proceeded to do exactly that.

"Taffy, this is...?"

"Keegan." He also crouched. "Hello Taffy."

The woman guided the dog over. "She's my beast. Whom I adore," she quickly added.

I grinned as I met Foster's gaze.

Taffy made her way over to Keegan.

"You're so pretty."

The dog cocked her head.

Keegan held out his hand.

Clearly, despite the fact their condo didn't allow any pets, the kids had learned how to approach strange dogs.

Once Keegan was petting Taffy, the woman stood and offered her hand to me. "Stephanie."

"Jai."

We shook.

"Jai went to school with Arnav." Foster grinned. "He's recently come back into my husband's life, and he's tickled. Oh, Arnav is." Clearly he felt clarification was necessary.

"I'm tickled as well. It's nice to reconnect with good parts of my past."

"So you're from Mission City?" Stephanie smiled, her bright-blue eyes shining. "I am as well. Oh, and my brother Cooper. We were well behind Arnav in school, though."

"Hey, babe... Oh." A lovely redheaded woman stepped from the kitchen. She wiped her hands on her jeans and pointed to herself. "Taryn."

"My wife." Stephanie grinned.

I cocked my head. "You were on your honeymoon at the beginning of the month. That's when I met Taffy."

The dog woofed.

Both women laughed. "Uh, yes." Taryn smiled. "My girl doesn't always love strangers, but she seems good with your two."

Before I could correct the assumption, Foster met my gaze. "Maybe you should introduce them?"

I laughed. A little awkwardly. "Yes. These are Demetrius's son and daughter—Keegan and Alaina."

Neither child looked up—both were clearly enthralled with the dogs.

Stephanie turned to Taryn. "Did you need something?"

"I was just going to head next door to grab the marinade. I completely forgot it."

"I can go." Stephanie gestured to the door.

Taryn shook her head. "You have fun with the pooches. I'll be right back." Carefully, she slipped past everyone and out the front door.

Neither dog attempted to follow her.

I apologized, "We're interrupting—" Obviously some kind of meal.

"Not at all." Stephanie glanced at Foster. "Sorry, it's your house. I shouldn't just be making myself at home."

He grinned. "You're family." He pivoted back to me. "Does everyone eat chicken or beef? I mean, unless you have other plans..."

My mouth sort of dropped open.

Stephanie pressed a hand to Foster's arm, but held my gaze. "We're inviting you for dinner. My brother Cooper and Taryn's brother Lachlan—who are now a couple and wow that's a crazy story—were supposed to come over, but they got caught up in doing some renovation thing. They're getting ready to sell Cooper's house and buying a bigger one, but they decided to just push through and finish the flooring. It'll take them until about midnight at the rate they're going, so they bailed on us. We have enough food for ten."

Foster waved. "We always cook way too much and love sharing." He gave me a meaningful look.

"I'll have to check with Demetrius." I directed my gaze meaningfully at the kids. "Not my call."

"Well, I want to stay." Alaina didn't break her loving gaze at Queenie. "Like, forever. Oh!" Now she did look up. "We're buying the house down the street." She pointed.

"The Singhs's?" Stephanie nearly squealed.

"Demetrius is putting in an offer." I was quick to make the correction, lest anyone think this was a done deal.

"Wow." Foster slowly smiled. "We'll be neighbors." He cocked his head. "You and..." He winced.

"Dad and Jai are a couple." Keegan grinned. "Jai's moving in." He frowned. "How does that work with camp?"

I swallowed the lump in my throat. "We haven't worked out the details. I'll need to stay at camp while the campers are there. Possibly during the entire summer season."

"But we'll see you, right?" Alaina pursed her lips. "I haven't even seen this place."

"You might." Keegan again smiled. "They're thinking about a camp with siblings of queer kids. Right?"

I blinked. "Well, yes. That's under consideration for next year." But we hadn't told anyone.

"Alessandra." Keegan shrugged, as if sensing my confusion. "She said something about it. I think it's a great idea."

"That's right." Alaina nodded. "I said it would be cool."

Stephanie cocked her head.

"I'm gay." Keegan puffed out his chest. "That's how Jai and Dad met. Jai's the director of the camp."

Will we ever tell the kids we knew each other from before? That'll be up to Demetrius. We wouldn't tell them about What'sUp Pup, of course. But perhaps...no. Although I'd always have fond memories of my pup time at the club, my relationship with Demetrius started the day...what? He showed up at camp? The night we ate at Stavros's? Last evening? I just didn't know.

A knock sounded at the door.

Taffy started yapping.

"Oh, hush you." Stephanie petted the dog while Foster moved to the front door.

Demetrius stood there, hands in his pockets.

"Lovely." Foster grinned. "We were just asking if the kids eat chicken and beef."

"Because we're staying for dinner," Alaina declared. "So we can play with the dogs."

"Yeah." Keegan's contribution.

Demetrius blinked. "We love chicken and beef."

"That's good. Would you mind stepping inside?" Taryn's disembodied voice came from behind him.

He stepped inside and out of her way.

"I'm Taryn. This is my wife, Stephanie. I understand you've met our dog. Welcome." She sailed past and into the kitchen.

Stephanie laughed. "You know, when I met her, she was a little shy. Cooper and I cured her of that." She eyed Demetrius. "My older brother. A bit of an enthusiastic freight train."

"You have to show Demetrius your engagement video." Foster nudged her.

"Oh yes." She again nearly squealed. "I brought a ring, and Taryn— Oh, let's keep it a surprise. We can show it to you on Foster's big screen."

I smiled. "I would love that." I was finding this woman, with her obvious enthusiasm, positively charming. "And you live on the street?"

"Yep. Right next door. Always available to babysit."

"I don't need a babysitter." Alaina glared.

"Okay." Stephanie's smile didn't waver. "I never wanted one either. My big brother Cooper took care of me."

Keegan puffed out his chest. "I take care of her."

Alaina rolled her eyes.

A feeling of rightness settled in my chest. *Can things really be this easy? I get the man of my dreams? The Daddy I always wanted? The partner I never dreamed I'd have?*

As if sensing my thoughts, Demetrius snagged my hand.

Foster sighed.

"Hey, what's going on in here?" Arnav entered from the kitchen. "Oh, you're the guests Taryn was telling me about. Great." He pointed to Demetrius. "You're helping me barbecue. We have chicken and beef kebobs. With green peppers and onions." He nodded toward the kids.

"Onions are my favorite. I'm Alaina. Are you his husband?" She pointed to Foster.

"He's Foster." Demetrius eyed me.

I couldn't remember who all had been introduced. I said simply, "Dogs."

He laughed. "Fair enough."

Five hours later, Alaina and Keegan were hunkered down in the enby dorm because it was smaller than the other dorms—Alaina thinking camp was the coolest thing ever and Keegan feeling very grown-up giving her the tour.

Demetrius and I were in my cabin, with our phones on our respective nightstands. We'd be able to hear the kids shout, of course, but we were also a phone call or text away. Alaina was just a year younger than our youngest camper, and Keegan knew the ropes. I was pretty certain I was more nervous than Demetrius was.

Of course, I'd passed all this by Alessandra who had enthused.

A huge parcel of assumptions went into that statement.

That I'd still be with the family next year.

That I'd be camp director next year.

That it'd be okay for me to be camp director while Keegan and, and possibly Alaina, attended their respective camps.

That it was okay for me to have Demetrius stay with me another night.

Oh, and she was thrilled to hear the offer for the house had been accepted. Demetrius was contacting his mortgage person Monday, and the house inspector was also coming that day.

Demetrius had just made slow, languid love to me.

This time, we cleaned up right away—in case the kids needed us.

He held me in his arms. "You know, I'm not even sure I asked you to move in."

I stilled.

"Oh, it's what I want. It's what the kids want. They told me when you and Stephanie were cleaning the dishes. Then they went off to play with Taryn, Arnav, and the dogs."

I chuckled. "You know you're committed to getting a dog, right?"

"Cadence sent me Torah Dixon's information. The trainer. Foster mentioned hearing about a bonded pair of schnauzers."

"Pair?" My mind raced.

"Well, each kid would have their own dog. I mean, they hardly ever fight, but it would be nice to, I don't know, give them each the responsibility. The house is big enough." He snuggled me closer. "It's going to be tough to find time to play, but..."

"But...?"

"Don't be mad."

"I could never be mad at you." Well, that might've been an exaggeration. Him dropping his bombshell on the kids—if it had gone sideways—would've annoyed me. He'd barely confirmed we were together when he sprang it on the kids. On the other hand, better to deal with the fallout right away rather than let things fester.

Keegan had taken me aside and given me the *don't hurt my dad* speech.

I'd nearly cried—all the while holding it together because I'd been aware of Demetrius's gaze on us. I wouldn't tell him Keegan's precise words—those were between the young man and me—but I'd eventually share the sentiments.

"You say that now..."

I twisted in his arms so I faced him. I was incredibly grateful Alessandra had seen fit to make this bed a king—my new man took up a lot of space. "What do you mean?"

"Well...Foster and I were talking..."

"You two get on like a house on fire. I think it's great." And I did. My rekindled friendship with Arnav meant a lot to me—that Demetrius and Foster were growing close did my heart good. Made me happy.

"And apparently I have something in common with Arnav. And you have something in common with Foster."

I blinked.

We'd left one light on, but the light cast deep shadows.

"What are you trying to say?" Because I couldn't figure out—

"Foster's a pup."

"Excuse me?" I gawped.

"You heard me. Arnav's a Daddy and Foster's a pup."

My eyes widened. "Oh my God. How did *that* come up in conversation?"

"We were discussing the responsibilities of taking care of pets, and Foster made a quip about keeping his toys away from Queenie." Demetrius chuckled. "I swear he started blushing. Then I said I knew a few pups and casually asked if he had a bed he liked to use. He nodded and said he kept it under the bed he shared with Arnav. And I suggested I should get tips for the caring and love of pups from Arnav."

"You didn't tell—"

"Nope. Absolutely not. And Foster didn't ask." He closed one eye. "Although he did muse about you taking off that first night after giving the dog treats to Queenie and Taffy."

My cheeks heated. "I forgot about that."

"I didn't say anything then either. I couldn't tell if you were being literal—as in there are two dogs here—or if you were trying to say something. After you took off, I figured I'd just keep my mouth shut."

"Odds are Foster's recounting this story to Arnav right now."

"That's entirely possible."

"And Arnav's putting together the pieces."

"Uh…"

"Discretion isn't your strong suit, sometimes."

"No. Sorry. But…you know…Foster made the comment."

"And you think he was sensing he'd get a receptive audience."

"I honestly don't know. I mean, I didn't get a pup vibe from him, and I didn't get a Daddy vibe from Arnav…but if I'd seen them in another context, I probably would've seen something."

"Because once you see it, you can't unsee it." I understood what he was saying. I also thought I might have a super difficult time facing my friend again. *Yeah, except if your mother told everyone, they know anyway.*

I pushed the pup topic aside, for now. "I feel like I should be contributing more."

He blinked. "Uh… We were talking about Arnav and Foster…"

"And I moved on to the subject of your new house. And, for the record, Foster said he was barely able to contribute anything to their down payment, and Arnav didn't care."

"Well, he wouldn't be the man I'm coming to know and respect if that had been an impediment."

"I have virtually nothing."

"Jai—"

"No, let me say this. I don't even own furniture. If not for Alessandra and Smith's kindness, I wouldn't have a place to live. I've worked low-paid jobs—"

"Important jobs."

"—and I have almost nothing to show for it."

"Okay." He cupped my cheek. "Buttercup, most of what I have is because of Erlene. I spent any theoretical inheritance I might've had after Nan died, to take care of my sisters. I was starting to build some savings when Erlene and I found each other. She needed me. That we have money now is because of her life-insurance policy. This house will be the kids' legacy. I'll keep saving for their education, of course. And—"

I placed a finger to his lips. "I want to contribute. I don't know...pay rent or something. I've got a good salary. And now benefits and contributions to a pension. Alessandra is a very generous employer. I'm also free to take other work during the downtimes."

"She's also willing to pay for you to retrain." He held my gaze.

"I like being a financial analyst. Putting that degree to good use—it's what got me the job." I shrugged. "What else would I do?"

"Whatever you like. That's her point. Or keep doing what you're doing. There are probably other nonprofits that could use your expertise. I'm just trying to say that you don't have to feel obliged to contribute to our household."

I blinked. "Gary..."

"The Gnat."

"Yes...."

"I'm not judging you for being with him, by the way. I'm judging him for being a total jackass."

I smiled. "Thank you for that." I drew in a deep breath. "I'd been contributing, and he still kept everything."

"Which is one of the reasons I'm saying you need to build your own nest egg."

"Am I your partner? I feel like we're moving so fast."

He nodded. "Sorry. I'm a bit of a freight train. Would you like to be my boyfriend?"

"Yes." I nodded frantically.

"Would you like to move in with me and the kids? No pressure."

Right...like the kids weren't already set on this course. Another nod. "Yes, I would like that." I stilled. "You realize I don't *have* to move in, right?" I needed him to see I wasn't helpless or homeless.

He cocked his head.

"You're always coming in and rescuing people. You think you love me because you see me as damaged. As needing rescue."

"No, I don't."

"Are you sure?" I held still.

"Oh." He furrowed his brow. "You think I'm saying I love you because I think you need to be rescued, and that I think it's love because I can save you." He rubbed his forehead. "That makes my head hurt."

"I'm saying even if I don't move in with you, that I'll be okay. I've come to grips with what happened. I have to say—it helps to know Gary's in jail for a long time." I smiled. "And I love you, too. I think I might've even back then. God knew, when I thought of my future, I wanted an egalitarian relationship most of the time...but also someone I could be a pup with." I pressed my hand to his cheek. "I just can't believe I found you again. And, to be clear, again, I'm telling you that I love you, too. Probably always have and definitely always will. Keegan and Alaina are a bonus. I never thought I'd have kids—"

"And now you're basically signing up to co-parent. If you want."

"I want." I chuckled. "I think they're onboard with that as well."

"They are."

"And dogs."

"And dogs."

"We're going to be very busy."

He pressed a kiss to my forehead. "We'll figure this out. We just have to keep the lines of communication open."

"Yep." I stilled.

"What?"

"How do you...?" I cleared my throat. "How do you envision the pup thing happening? I put that side of me away for a very long time, and I didn't do well with that. I've found my Daddy...but the kids come first."

"Yeah." He toyed with my hair. "We're not going to tell them—"

"Uh, no."

"But I agree we need time together as Daddy and pup."

"Yes."

He rubbed my shoulder. "The kids are away at school. I work from home on a flexible schedule. I don't know about you..."

"Obviously I can't get away when we have campers."

"That's a given."

"But I've got a flexible schedule as well. I'm okay with Daddy/pup time while the kids are at school. Also..." I met his gaze. "I would love to go to a pup night if there is such a thing these days. You could hang out with the Daddies while I get to do puppy piles." Excitement grew within me. Then a little impishness. "Do you think Arnav and Foster would be interested in joining us? Because once you see something, you kind of can't unsee it."

He guffawed. "That's true. And yes, I'll ask Arnav." He smiled. "We can make this work." He scratched my scalp. "I love you, pup."

"I love you, Daddy. I'm amazed you're still awake."

He arched an eyebrow, then laughed. "It's been a struggle—but you're worth it." He rolled onto his back and pulled me into his side.

I ran my hand through his chest hair. "I didn't know I could be this happy."

"You'll always be my priority, Jai. You and the kids."

"And I get to take care of you?"

"I wouldn't complain." He yawned.

I reached over to flip off the lamp.

Within moments, his breathing evened.

Much later, mine did as well.

Chapter Twenty-Four

Demetrius

"Stop fidgeting. You look amazing."

Jai pursed his lips.

"I think you look handsome." I eyed his brilliant-blue sherwani with its intricate silver thread. "You're doing this for Arnav."

"Ha." Jai rolled his eyes. "He probably won't even be here."

"Want to bet?" I arched an eyebrow.

"He's here." Another eye roll.

"And he looks just as good as you." Arnav's sherwani was a deep burgundy and suited him. Foster held his arm and grinned.

He probably feels as lucky as I do.

"You knew he was going to be here." I feathered Jai's hair.

He bristled.

I grinned. "This is Rashmi's shindig." Arnav's sister had organized this fundraiser for a not-for-profit language school she was opening.

For which Jai had done all the accounting. Once the school was up and running, he would be able to put it into caretaker mode. It would require an hour or two a week and more during tax filing season.

Alessandra and Smith, thrilled with the project, had donated money. They were in attendance this afternoon—Smith in a tux and Allie in a shimmering silver ball gown. Truly, they were the fanciest dressed in the room.

Arnav and Rashmi's sister Beena had worn jeans.

Most of the guests were somewhere in the middle.

I'd dug out a suit, had it dry cleaned, and now tried to look grown up.

Keegan and Alaina were in the playroom with Arnav's more than a dozen nibblets. Parvan, now a confidant of Keegan's, was helping corral the masses. How Arnav kept them all straight was beyond me.

"I'm glad Stephanie and Taryn are watching Gus and Gizmo." Jai brushed at his sleeve.

"Jesus, stop fidgeting. Yes, the dogs are better off with Taffy and Queenie." Gus was Alaina's dog while Gizmo had bonded to Keegan instantly.

Torah was keeping every member of our family busy learning how to train these two wonderful—but incredibly obstinate—schnauzers.

School was starting next week, and the kids were ready. Keegan was even talking about getting a part-time job—since he was of legal age to work. I got the feeling he wanted to *contribute*. He was growing up way too fast. If he did work, I'd encourage him to save for either college or a car—or both.

Alaina, for her part, wanted to operate a dog-walking business.

Jai was taking her through how to start that up so she'd be ready—when she turned twelve—to launch her venture.

"What are *you* doing here?" A cultured woman's voice caught my attention.

Jai stiffened.

Well, this isn't going to be good.

Together, we turned to face an older Indian couple. Despite the gray hair and slightly stooped stature, I had no doubt I was facing Jai's father. And, therefore, likely his mother as well.

"Hello Mother. Father." Jai did a weird head bob.

"Why are you here?" Her voice was a little shrill, and her scowl didn't match the happiness of her vibrant pink sari.

"Rashmi invited me. You remember I'm friends with Arnav?" He pressed his hand to my arm. "May I present my boyfriend? This is Demetrius Fulton. Demetrius, these are my parents, Mr. and Mrs. Prasad."

"That boy was a bad influence on you. Look how you turned out."

Apparently she was simply going to ignore me. That was fine—I didn't care for her much either. But, red flashed before my eyes. How dare she insult two men I cared for deeply? Jai, obviously. We were headed to the altar in the not-too-distant future. The sooner the better, as far as I was concerned. As well, Foster and Arnav had become dear friends. We went back and forth between our houses all the time—them claiming they needed practice parenting. For which Keegan and Alaina were mighty pleased to get the extra attention.

Which gave Jai and me desperately needed alone time as we worked to establish a relationship that worked for both of us.

Before I could react, though, she continued. "Does this one know you pretend to be a dog and like it?"

My jaw dropped.

Jai's cheeks turned dark crimson.

I cleared my throat. "Oh yes. Jai is my beloved pup. And since you're his mother, I guess that makes you a bitch. I ask you to steer clear of Jai and my family. We don't need people like you in our lives. Good day." I grasped Jai's arm and guided him away from the two people who were supposed to love him the most in the world. "Jesus Christ, is she always that bad?" I'd maneuvered us right out of the hall and into the bright daylight. The water reflected off the water, as we were down at the wharf.

A long silence followed, and I worried Jai might be in trouble, but he started laughing.

"You just called my mother a bitch."

"Uh..." I winced. "Sometimes I speak before I think. It's a fault of mine."

He shook his head. "That was fucking brilliant. I could never have done that...but I'll never regret that you had the courage to. I've been worried about what might happen when I ran into them. Mission City is small enough that it's bound to happen." He grinned. "And now I know. I'll just remind her she's a bitch, and he's..." He frowned.

"The bitch's husband." I wrinkled my nose. "Or something. Oh, I know. We'll ask Arnav—he has the best lines." While Foster was placid, Arnav could stand up to anyone. With all those sisters, as well as a thriving law practice, he'd had plenty of experience.

"What if..." He winced. "What if one of the kids overheard? What if they tease Alaina and Keegan?"

I sighed. "That's a legitimate concern. No one was near us when we spoke. If your mother insists on telling everyone, there's not much we can do except be honest with the kids. I hope, though, that my comment gives her pause. There'll be blowback, and it'll hit them right in the face. You know Arnav's not going to put up with that shit either."

He pursed his lips. "The kids."

"Will always be our top priority, Buttercup." I feathered his hair and used his nickname since we were alone. "We'll deal with this when and if it comes up. Personally, I'm just fine with my kids never knowing what we're up to in our own time." I pressed a kiss to his temple.

"Is all okay here?" A tall Black man in jeans, a T-shirt, and a windbreaker approached.

I cocked my head.

"Oh, I'm Isaac. The harbormaster. I did the setup for the event, and then I'll hang around in the background until it's over." He shrugged. "I apologize for intruding—"

I stuck out my hand. "Demetrius. And this is my boyfriend, Jai."

Isaac shook first my hand, then Jai's.

"Do you ever hold wedding receptions here? Heck, maybe even the ceremony?" Jai held the man's gaze.

"If you want something small, we can certainly do that. There are larger venues—"

"No." Jai shook his head. "This place is perfect. Small. Intimate. On the water. At sunset, I think."

I blinked several times. "Yes. Just a few close friends."

"We have openings for that." Isaac eyed us. "For yourselves?"

We nodded.

I grinned. "So, I guess that makes us fiancés."

"Yeah." A grin spread across Jai's face. "I guess that does."

"Think Arnav and Foster will stand up for us?" Excitement rose within me. "Of course, Stephanie, Taryn, Alessandra, and Smith need to come."

"And Kennedy, Cody, Grey, and Makenna."

"Of course." His camp family had warmly embraced my family, and we'd all celebrated when the last camp group had gone home last week.

"I know a celebrant, if you need one." Isaac smiled.

"Oh, do you allow dogs? I'd love if Gus and Gizmo could come." More excitement at the prospect of making our family complete.

The harbormaster nodded. "My dog Buddy frequently visits me at work. With my husband Ben, of course."

I squinted. "Okay, that wouldn't be Ben the French Immersion teacher at Cedar Street Elementary, would it?"

Isaac's face broke into the widest grin I'd ever seen. "Why yes, that's my husband. Damn fine teacher. Great guy. You have kids in the school?"

"Our daughter is starting next week. We're new in town. Well, I am. Jai's newly come home."

"Ben and I were new to town when we arrived a few years ago. Mission City is a great place to raise kids."

"*Our daughter.*" Jai repeated the words.

I nodded.

He turned to Isaac. "We have two amazing kids."

"What are their names? How old are they?" He grinned. "I love kids. I mean, unless... You don't need to return to the party?"

Jai shook his head. "We'll collect the kids when it's time to leave. So Alaina's eleven going on thirty..." He continued on for several minutes about our kids.

Isaac asked insightful and kind questions—truly curious about our two.

I let the words wash over me as I gazed out over the bright blue of the Fraser River. I might not have brought Keegan to Mission City—and Pride Camp—with the intention of finding a new home...but we had. I gripped Jai's arm as he talked about Torah training the dogs and how wonderful life was.

I had to keep blinking so I wouldn't cry. I told myself the reflection of the sun off the water was the cause.

In truth, I just hadn't realized that, in finding my Buttercup, I'd find my happily ever after as well.

But I had.

Epilogue

Jai

F oster and I tugged each end of the rope.

I snarled. In fun.

He yipped his displeasure at me taking his toy.

You snooze, you lose. I yanked harder.

Foster, who built his muscles working construction, yanked back.

I lost my grip.

He grabbed the damn thing in his mouth and bounded over to his Daddy.

Arnav petted him with pride shining in his eyes.

My Daddy beckoned me over.

On all fours, I slunk over to him. Dejected I'd lost that round. *It's okay, I'll win next time.* All in fun, though. Having Foster as a friend was a highlight in my life.

Stephanie and Taryn were watching the kids at our house. With all four dogs in attendance, of course.

Just like we regularly took care of Taffy because, honestly, she was a great dog. And then Queenie invariably tagged along.

I pressed myself against Daddy's leg and accepted a drink of water.

"How are you gentlemen doing this evening?" Master Dante wore black trousers, a black silk shirt, and a wide smile.

His submissive, Evan, stood a respectful distance behind.

Their third, Mistress Kate, was whipping a misbehaving—but very willing—pup against the St. Andrew's Cross.

All was well at Club Kink.

In investigating What'sUp Pup, I'd discovered that club had closed, but Pup Night had been folded into an ongoing event at Kink.

Arnav and Foster had met here.

Sort of.

One night, they'd confessed they'd gone upstairs at a Halloween party and gotten into all kinds of mischief. Foster had panicked, though, and had fled.

The next month, they'd both wound up here.

And the rest was Daddy/pup history.

I sat at Daddy's feet with my kneepads and a leash attached to my collar. Naked, of course. I was happiest this way.

Foster sat beside Arnav, much as I was. He was older than me by more than fifteen years, but admitted he was happiest with his collar and at Arnav's side.

"All is well." My Daddy offered Dante a huge grin. "We're just eyeing the puppy pile."

So far, about ten pups were playing and having fun. I loved the pile because I didn't have any pressures. I could just have fun. I planned to join once I'd taken a break.

"A good turnout tonight. Oh, I see someone new arrived. If you'll excuse me...?"

We four nodded.

Curious, I turned to see who had arrived.

My jaw dropped. "Daddy?"

"Yes, Buttercup?"

"Is that Cody?"

Daddy turned. "Well, that's interesting. I have to admit I didn't see this coming."

Neither had I.

I was very intrigued why the camp psychologist was here on puppy night.

But whether Cody was a pup, a Daddy in training, or just curious about kink, was a minor curiosity. What truly mattered was that I was here, with my Daddy, the happiest I'd ever been. My life was complete.

Want to know why Cody is at pup night? Check out my next Daddy/pup book! Coming soon: A Daddy for Christmas 3: Lorcan

Need Arnav and Foster's Daddy/pup story? Check out A Daddy for Christmas 2: Foster (Love in Mission City Book 3.5

Want Aaron and Noel's story? Find in here in Love Without Reservations

Want more Dickens and Spike? Curious about Isaac the harbor master and his husband Ben? Both couples' stories are in Love in Mission City: The Shorts

Want Smith and Alessandra's story? Check out my dark erotic BDSM book (written under my pen name Gabbi Black) Beautiful Eyes

Want more Gabbi Grey?

Check out my Love in Mission City series, set in beautiful British Columbia.

The first book is

Ginger Snapping All the Way (Love in Mission City Book 1)

Also available:

Stanley's Christmas Redemption(Love in Mission City Book 2)

The Beauty of the Beast (Love in Mission City Book 2.5)

Sleigh Bells and Second Chances (Love in Mission City Book 3)

A Daddy for Christmas 2: Foster (Love in Mission City Book 3.5)

Rayne's Return (Love in Mission City Book 4)

Gideon's Gratitude (Love in Mission City Book 5)

Love in Mission City: The Boyfriend Gamble

Love in Mission City: The Boyfriends Duet

Love in Mission City: The Shorts

Rayne Check

Archer's Awakening

Leo's Lust

Thought You Were the One

Love Without Reservations

Page Against the Machine

The Lightkeeper's Love Affair

Ace's Place

Marcus's Cadence

Not in it for the Money

Also:

Axe to Grind

Grindstone's Edge

Voice to Raise

Hugh (Single Dads of Gaynor Beach)

Anthony (Single Dads of Gaynor Beach)

Xavier (Single Dads of Gaynor Beach)

Love Furever (Friends of Gaynor Beach Animal Rescue)

Husky Love (Friends of Gaynor Beach Animal Rescue)

Yorkie to My Heart (Friends of Gaynor Beach Animal Rescue)

My Past, Your Future

If Only for Today

Catch a Tiger by the Tail

Solstice Surprise

Valentino in Vancouver

You See Me

Sun, Surf, and Surprises

Ginger in the City

Caressa's Homecoming (Bound by Love Book 1)

Cole's Reckoning (Bound by Love Book 2)

An Uncommon Gentleman

A Sensible Gentleman

Didn't See You Coming

Finding Noah (Foggy Basin Season 2)

Unlocked and Unlost

Hot Rucking Canadian

Big Rucking Disaster

Audiobooks

Ginger Snapping All the Way

Stanley's Christmas Redemption

Sleigh Bells and Second Chances

Rayne's Return

Gideon's Gratitude

Rayne Check

Archer's Awakening

Thought You Were the One

Love in Mission City: The Shorts

Page Against the Machine

The Lightkeeper's Love Affair

Ace's Place

Marcus's Cadence

Not in it for the Money

Hugh (Single Dads of Gaynor Beach)

Anthony (Single Dads of Gaynor Beach)

Love Furever (Friends of Gaynor Beach Animal Rescue)

Husky Love (Friends of Gaynor Beach Animal Rescue)

My Past, Your Future

If Only for Today

Catch a Tiger by the Tail

Solstice Surprise

An Uncommon Gentleman

A Sensible Gentleman

Didn't See You Coming

Want a free short story? The story is set in Gaynor Beach, California where there are plenty of single dads and puppy rescues! You can sign up for my newsletter so you can keep up with all the great stuff I'm doing as well as pictures of my own pooches, Ally and Finnegan.

Hemingway's Happy Day

Love contemporary MF romances? What's better than love in the beautiful Cedar Valley in British Columbia, Canada? Find small town romances with a touch of angst, a bit of heat, and a lot of heart...

The Absolution of Abigail Reardon (prequel)

The Luminosity of Loriana Harper (Book 1)

The Making of Marnie Jones (Book 2)

The Redemption of Remy St. Claire (Book 3)

Interested in knowing more about Gabbi?

Sign up for her newsletter
Follow her on Bookbub
Follow her on Instagram

USA Today Bestselling author Gabbi Grey lives in beautiful British Columbia where her fur baby chin-poo keeps her safe from the nasty neighborhood squirrels. Working for the government by day, she spends her early mornings writing contemporary, gay, sweet, and dark erotic BDSM romances. While she firmly believes in happy endings, she also believes in making her characters suffer before finding their true love. She also writes m/f romances as Gabbi Black and Gabbi Powell.